Looking back on that amazing da[...] Nevada in April of 1986, I had no [...] as far as the paranormal is concer[...]. Who would have guessed? I was a waitress working at NAS Fallon, and John was a newly enlisted jet mechanic on a det in our town with the Navy.

Ghosts and the paranormal were a topic with it's own special designated class that wasn't approached until we had our first joint encounter as a married couple. Considering that we both have October birthdays very near Halloween you would have thought that ghosts, spirits, and unexplained phenomena would have been foremost on our minds, but being newly married took center stage up until my first visit to John's family home in Pennsylvania.

Being seekers of all things paranormal, my family and I are continually asked about our belief in ghosts and whether or not we have seen a ghost or experienced paranormal activity. The answer is yes to all of these questions. We have lived with the unexplained since as far back as each of us can remember. My husband, John grew up in a house in the borough of Newell, Pennsylvania where ghosts and poltergeists harbored for his entire childhood. That house is still the center of many unexplained events and situations.

Our encounters with the paranormal has escalated into the double digits as far as counting our paranormal episodes goes, so I will put the year with the place that the occurrence with the other side happened and share some of our family's experiences with ghosts, even though in the past we have attempted to keep them guarded from friends, co-workers, and acquaintances as much as humanly possible. I am merely a novice writer attempting to share our true experiences with the paranormal, so please excuse the bad grammar, spelling and punctuation that may arise from time to time.

Newell, Pennsylvania 1986: I have had my share of surprise encounters with the supernatural, but nothing quite as extreme when compared with the things that were buried deep in that antiquated home that my husband grew up in. Not long after moving to Virginia Beach from Fallon, Nevada, to be with John, who was currently stationed with the Navy, we drove to his hometown of Newell, Pennsylvania so that I could meet his family. The old house was full of surprises that included ornery ghosts and other entities that I was unfamiliar with at that time.

Today, I now know that I was dealing poltergeists. I would be upstairs when disembodied voices that resembled John's siblings would call out my name even though they were nowhere near the home. At night once the house was quiet, red eyes would peer at you from the upstairs near the corner of the closet. Disembodied footsteps would run up and down the steps.

Built in 1900, the haunted and historic home is located at the corner of 4th Street, just across the street from the old railroad tracks and the town's Honor Roll where the military banners proudly display of all of those who served. The Granato family purchased the home during the early sixties. They were completely unaware that the house held a sorted history that involved ghosts and paranormal activity that no child should ever have to live with.

Not long after moving in the haunted dwelling, the patriarch of the family, Louis Granato felt that things were not quite right and immediately detected paranormal activity in the two-story home, even though the supernatural activity was in it's infancy at that time. Despite the lack of modern day information involving the paranormal, it quickly became obvious to Mr. and Mrs. Granato that a very dark and ominous secret lay hidden deep within the depths of the cellar, looming in the darkness, threatening to implode with each visit to the gloomy and menacing perimeter that lay underneath the ground floor.

Frightening and over-powering shadows overcast the cellar with the hint of threat to anyone who dared to unearth it, making it a forceful entity that would not be easily understood. When the large and domineering shadow became evident to family members who would periodically witness the unexplainable creature, it would appear to be mimicking that of a large rabid feline raging war with the human race in a diabolic way that forced the family to stay away from the threatening and evil space that posed many questions and little to no answers.

Due to a fear of the unknown, the need to relocate the laundry-room from the cellar was obvious. Just above the entrance to the cellar-way, in the heart of the residence was a very open and a large room that allowed for the children to have a play area as well as accommodate modern appliances that allowed for the family to interact and have a common space is still known today as the playroom.

The cellar was not an exclusive spot in the house where paranormal activity was concerned. While living in or visiting the home you always had the feeling that you were never alone. Unexplained noises, orbs and heavy footsteps descending the stairs when you least expected it became a normal part of the home's atmosphere and the center for supernatural occurrences.

The feeling of being watched was not a phenomenon that the family was used to prior to moving into the 4th Street Residence, but it was prevalent, even though the reason was never quite made clear. Several rumors surrounding the house surfaced from well-meaning neighbors, but the thought of dead bodies being buried in the cellar was the very thing that sent the imaginations of developing adolescent minds flying.

The upper half of the Granato home became an even larger consideration where supernatural influences were concerned. The cellar's dark and eerie shadow issue made the family second guess what was going on with their new residence and was nothing compared to what was about to rear it's ugly head. Demonic red eyes peering at the children in the still of the night, and a chimney packed full of black birds that erupted during an episode when the oldest daughter walked into the room.

The one light at the end of this paranormal tunnel of horrors was a small blond ghost child that appeared during times of illness, sadness and uncertainty. Her presence was a safe haven and most assuring was the unspoken promise to the person witnessing her sweet, childlike spirit was that they were nothing less than safe.

Disembodied voices would call family members names, beckoning them to come see what the ghostly caller wanted, only to discover that nobody was calling them at all, at least no one that could be seen, but the voices, divest of human existence resembled those of family members, leading to ambivalent feelings of a distorted universe that was now the place that they called their home.

Nightmares quickly became part of the Granato children's night time regiment, and at times, scratches appeared on their extremities and were discovered in the morning hours when preparing for school. No rational explanation as to what was occurring could be found, and the dark shadows, unexplained activity and strange anomalies would continue on throughout the history of the occupants who continue to live there today.

Lou, the oldest Granato child had a love of art and would often display his passion on the walls of the upstairs bedroom with demonic illustrations. Futile attempts of removing the malevolent creatures proved to be a tedious chore of continuously painting the obstructed area to little or no avail. The demonic images were much stronger than anticipated and reared their ugly heads despite countless gallons of paint covering their distressing and hostile sub-terrestrial lifeforms.

What can only be explained as severely energetic poltergeist action would come to life at any given moment to in the kitchen and dining area with a flux of activity that included dishes flying through the air, strange odors, whispers, footsteps, and noises that could never be located despite their emanating from within the room. Horrifying images of transparent ghostly faces would show themselves through the large picture window of the home's living-room even though it stood approximately eight-feet from the ground outside, making it virtually impossible for a normal human to cause such an anomaly.

Today, a new generation of Granato family members resides in the home that never sleeps. The stories aren't as dark as they once were, but the paranormal activity continues on. Fresh paint and new memories have renovated the home's atmosphere, but the past is permanently etched into the minds of generations before and can never quite be ignored as those who lived through the testimonies can attest, some things just stay with you no matter how hard you attempt to put them in your rear-view mirror.

Star Junction, Pennsylvania: Founded in 1893, Star Junction today is a quiet village with a population of roughly six-hundred people. The neighborhood consists of duplex style houses that was built for coal mining families. The village is located just off of highway 51 in Fayette County, between Perryopolis and Smock, Pennsylvania in an unincorporated community that sit's in the heart of Perry Township and was once home to a bustling coal mining center.

The beehive ovens came into place when the Washington No. 2 mine opened. The coke ovens can be seen nestled along the hillside just past the crossroads oh Route 51 and Main Street during the cooler months when the thick Pennsylvania foliage isn't blocking them from view.

Star Junction was at one time a popular site where a railroad depot, company store and over 4,000 miners worked from dawn to dusk. The "village" is filled with coal patch style company houses where families of those who once labored remains today. By day, Star Junction is quiet and unassuming, but nightfall brings a host of tales, legends and unexplained circumstances that only those who have experienced can tell in detail.

The darkness of the night never fails to emanate at precisely the right time during certain nights, and it is at these times that the mist envelopes the Star Junction, making visibility nearly null and void. At times during the blackness, evil would rear its ugly head in the form of unrecognizable entities that are shadowed from full view. The dark, black diabolical entities, and apparitions come across to the living as lifeless and void of all emotion. They appear to be in constant search of something that is no longer there.

Living in a small community on most days was uneventful. The town was sleepy, lacking of crime, and everyone was acquainted with their neighbors. During the day, people went about their business in a lively manner, planting flowers in the summer, shoveling snow in the winter, and catching crayfish down by the creek when the weather permitted.

We moved to Star Junction in early 2002 into a duplex that had once been inhabited by a family who had lived in the residence for more than a hundred years. Unaware to us, the house carried a history that we would eventually find hard to wrap our mind's around. More than just a little haunted, our house never tired of paranormal episodes, yet we somehow still managed to live in the house located on Main Street for just over a decade.

Our two younger daughters enrolled in Frazier and quickly made friends in the community. Our new home was soon bustling with activity. Sleepovers, birthday parties, family gatherings, and summer barbecues were a regular occurrence at our home. Unfortunately, so were the ghost sightings, paranormal encounters and unexplained events that would shape our life in a place that we never could have possibly envisioned. Our personal circumstances involving the paranormal soon escalated into the double digits as far as counting our episodes with ghosts goes.

We hadn't been in the house a week when our first paranormal encounter occurred. The girls had just stepped off of the bus and was walking through the kitchen door when our youngest daughter, Joni abruptly stopped and stared at the table. Later she asked me, "who the lady was that was sitting at the kitchen table with me drinking coffee." I responded to her in an inquisitive manner because I had had no visitor on that particular day. Curious, I then asked her to describe the woman. She told me that she had brown hair, a plaid shirt and large glasses. At the time we assumed that she had a severely overactive imagination and i summed up the episode as merely nothing more than my youngest attempting to mess with my mind.

A week later, we began to notice strange sounds and smells. The aroma of cherry pipe tobacco was prevalent. The feeling that we were not alone was strong, but at the same time, we felt safe despite the strange ambiances that the house was sending out. I unpacked our boxes and made the house as homey as I could. My modern decor clashed with the gold, green and brown of the home's antiquated furnishings, but I made the best of what I had to work with. I enrolled our two younger daughters in school and John found work, so it was just me and our oldest daughter in the house all day.

A few months later, we were informed by our landlord that his father, Ivan had passed away. He asked us if we would like to move over to the larger side of the duplex as it offered quite a bit more space and was modernized. We quickly agreed due to there being an extra bedroom, and the other side was completely furnished, including the contents of the cupboards, drawers, and the refrigerator.

Our landlord, Carl informed us that we were welcome to whatever we needed, but that if we found any papers, certificates, a long ago buried time capsule or something of importance to let him know. We soon discovered that the house was a treasure trove stuffed to the rafters with relics and antiques. After exploring, we found that the kitchen cupboards were a haven filled with several Tupperware bowls filled with silver quarters, two dollar bills, silver certificates, and letters of importance that included insurance beneficiaries. The attic held games and trinkets from the 1920s through the 1970s.

After informing our landlord that we had discovered the mother lode, he came and collected money and several family treasures that he had no clue had even existed. He had little interest in the vintage games or other things that had been left behind under layers of dust from another era. With his permission, we kept the vintage furniture, kitchen utensils and other embellishments that the prior occupant had used.

We later determined that this may have been our first mistake. Ghosts have a way of attaching themselves to beloved objects. After living in the Star Junction duplex for just a few months, we quickly learned just how powerful ghosts can be. True, they were harmless, and they appeared to welcome us into it, but they also made their point that this was their home.

We learned that power outages were a common thing, but we also learned that this was not a problem for us as far as morning was concerned. Someone would tap John on the shoulder when the alarm clock failed, waking him just in time for work. We would see ethereal images of a man dressed in a plaid shirt, sitting on the couch, reflected in the television screen when it was off. We would hear disembodied footsteps running from the upstairs, down into the kitchen all hours of the day and night.

Our names would be called, but never would someone answer when we replied. The strange odor of cherry pipe tobacco was stronger on this side of the duplex. The house was a three-story that had a cellar with a few dark rooms. One of those rooms had two deep freezers. One was packed with cherries and several frozen turkeys. There was also a personal stash of homemade wine that was endless. We opened one of the bottles, but were greeted with the foul stench of bitter grapes that had met their expiration.

The doors to the home had a way of opening by themselves, and the cellar was never at rest. The sound of bricks being chipped away by vintage tools and a restless ghost who had unfinished business resounded throughout the night. Orbs and a strange mist enveloped the cellar, and you always had the feeling that you were being watched. The dark, wet atmosphere led to coldness and an atmosphere of secrets hidden behind the cement walls that appeared to reach out in hushed whispers by the restless skeletons that inhabited the portals from days gone by where the past is attempting to inform the present.

Curious about our new and unexplained situation, we went to the next door neighbors to ask a variety of questions about the prior occupants of the house that we were now living in. They informed us that the lady who had lived there had died on Thanksgiving morning several years before. This gave us a reason as to why there were a half dozen turkeys in the deep freeze. Her husband bought one turkey each year, but just could not bring himself to roast it in light of his wife's passing on such a beloved holiday.

Through time, and after thoroughly searching the entire house, we had located a bundle of photos and a drawer full of silver certificates. Our youngest daughter could not help but to notice a photo of a dark haired lady dressed in a plaid shirt, who was wearing glasses. We called the landlord and informed him of the things that we had discovered.

Carl came to pick the family heirlooms up one afternoon. We asked him who the woman was in the photo. He told us that it was his mother, Bernice, who had passed on Thanksgiving morning. We learned that this was the female ghost who had sat with me when we lived on the other side of the duplex just six months prior.

The man of the house had fallen and broken his hip while changing the oil in his truck He had temporarily been placed in a care home, but had passed away due to complications from pneumonia. The couple, Bernice and Ivan had lived in the house for over fifty years. Prior to that, the house had belonged to her parents. The family had a deep history and they had no intentions of interrupting their lives, so they carried on as if they were still inhabiting the only home that they knew.

Once we learned of the couple's demise things really went out of bounds. We began to physically see what strong spirits are capable of performing in the afterlife. On Christmas day, my husband and oldest daughter, Jennifer were sitting on the couch when suddenly the living room door opened and slammed shut. The image of Ivan's reflection in the television was becoming a regular thing. We had no clue that this was just the beginning of things to come.

Star Junction was no stranger to unexplained deaths during our time living in the borough. While we only lived in the community for a decade, it did not go unnoticed that many of our neighbors passed away. Accidental deaths and suicides were at a fairly high range for one sleepy town, but then again, the patch had a reputation for never sleeping, and for such a small area, past and present, the death toll was a bit staggering.

The creek located behind our house, just past the ball field we soon learned was a hotbed for paranormal activity. We would see dark shadows, and the vivid images of a small white misty apparition that appeared to be that of a small child. After asking about the history of the area, we were informed that a young girl had drowned in the creek during the hiatus of the junctions booming coke ovens. Many families had moved to the area in search of work, making the town a prime location for new residents moving into the small community.

The creek held many secrets that included several supernatural events that our friends and family experienced while visiting. One night after cleaning up, a neighbor and myself witnessed a dark black shadow, seen through the kitchen window, totally engulfing the backyard in a way that was bone chilling, eerie and diabolical. The crickets were quickly silenced, replaced by a flapping noise that was not from this world, and the perimeter surrounding the rear of our home suddenly became cold and uninviting. A group of us witnessed a huge black mass that moved slowly through the yard and simply dissipated into thin air.

On another occasion, while sitting around the kitchen table, our middle daughter noticed the sound of a slight musical backdrop reminiscent of "lullaby music." Appearing slightly freaked out, Jessica asked her dad, siblings and myself if we could hear it. In unison we said, "no." Then, within seconds, all hell broke loose. We also began to hear the resounding harmony, slight as it was, of the lyrics, "lullaby, and good night." Then, without hesitation, the twelve windows that lined our mud room slammed shut in unison. This sudden anomaly gave us all a reason to jump out of our skin. Next, the apparition of a small man formed near the windows. Needless to say, we all came unglued at the hinges.

A few months later, we had a birthday party for our middle daughter, Jessica. They had invited several friends who continued to run up and down the stairs for most of the party. One particular guest who appeared to sense the turmoil revolving around our house noted that the ghosts were attempting to reach out to us in an effort to keep our family safe. After ascending the stairway, he quickly stopped at our bedroom door, turned and stared at the bed. Being sensitive to the deceased, Eric appeared to be in somewhat of a trance as he peered at our bed.

He then asked us how we could sleep in that room. We informed him that it was our bedroom. He then described a lady with dark hair who had passed away while in the bed, in that room, and that she was trying to warn me that I needed to stay out of that room or else I would get sick. Not long after this declaration was made I found myself in the hospital with adult onset asthma and pneumonia.

Driving into town on foggy nights, we often witnessed the sight of a shadow man, dressed in period clothing. His antiquated coat and boots appeared to be attire straight out of the 1800s. The horrifying image walked slowly along the edge of the ballfield, near the creek. As I slowed down the car to get a better look, we all would notice that the ghost man was void of a face, replaced by a blackened void of nothingness. Regardless of his having a lack of facial extremities, you could feel that he was peering back at you, delving straight through your soul and leaving a permanent mark that would not allow you to forget his presence.

Needless to say, we soon discovered that our time in this lovely, but very haunted abode had met it's deadline. The paranormal encounters were becoming too much for any of us to handle. Friends and family were getting freaked out by the regular paranormal encounters. Our daughters who had once loved sleepovers were afraid to ask their friends to spend the night due to never knowing what would happen from one day to the next. Our time had come to move on.

I would love to say that the paranormal encounters ended in Star Junction, but they have only gotten worse. Instead of fearing them, we have learned to embrace them. Our friends and family have witnessed many of these supernatural events with us and although it scares several of them, they understand that some things are beyond our control and totally inescapable. It has become apparent to us that the ghosts have a story to tell.

Star Junction is located in Fayette County, home to hundreds of historic buildings and sites, and the center of many haunted venues, homes and nearby towns. The haunted borough of Newell is just 9 miles down the scenic Central School country road, and the notably haunted and historic, Quaker Church and Cemetery is located along Quaker Church Road just a few miles away in Perryopolis Pennsylvania.

According to the most popular urban legend, this small cemetery dates back to the early 1700's and was founded by the Quaker pioneers. The paranormal hotspot was once used as the location for the practice of black magic. It is believed that the cemetery is haunted by dark spirits, as a result of this.

Sitting in the middle of the cemetery is the historic Quaker church. The small one room building is made of rough cut stone. Both the stone church and surrounding graveyard is known for being both cursed and haunted. There is writing on the walls inside of the building which describes how a person, who is buried outside died, and if you read the description of their death, you will die the same death as they did. Another misfortune has to do with one of the headstones being cursed, meaning that if you stand at the grave, walk over it , or read the poem inscribed on the stone, which begins by stating " Remember youth as you go by" you could have bad luck or worse.

Six miles south of Star Junction you will locate Allen's Haunted Farm & Hayrides in Smock, Pennsylvania. By their own admission, Allen's claims to be, "The world's first Haunted Hayride! For most people the hayride lasts 30 minutes, for others, it lasts a lifetime! A wagon departs every 15 minutes and travels into the darkness on Route 666 where you will travel through the darkened and eerie woods, corn fields and into the authenticated "Haunted Barn." The haunted venue also offers carnival rides, games & concessions. Allen's barn has been listed in Pennsylvania's 80 Haunted Sites.

Just up the road is another community surrounded by paranormal activity. Layton, Pennsylvania is a quiet, unincorporated locality in Fayette County that has two prominent ghost stories. The first one revolves around the Layton Bridge, which just so happens to be the only way to enter the town if you are driving from Star Junction or Perryopolis.

The bridge was built in 1899 and is reportedly haunted by a man who was walking along the tracks and got hit by an eastbound train ran by the Washington Railroad Company. With nowhere to run, the man was hit and dragged into the tunnel. His remains were later found halfway through the tunnel. Late on windy nights as you drive through the tunnel you can hear his anguished screams.

A portion of the movie, Silence of the Lambs was filmed in Layton, Pennsylvania at 8 Circle Street. As noted by realtor, Dianne Wilk, the 1910 Princess Anne home was chosen to be featured in the Silence of the Lambs movie due to the eerie qualities of taste and prosperity that it easily exhibited to those passing by. The house offers a near perfect expression of comfort with its wraparound veranda and a prominent staircase of paneled walls of oak.

Star Junction was added to the National Register of Historic Places in 1997. The reasons for the addition is that the district includes 163 contributing buildings and 2 contributing structures in the bituminous coal mining community. The majority of the buildings were built between 1892 and 1918, with 130 of the contributing buildings being two-story, frame duplex workers' housing.

The oldest building is the Whitsett farmhouse, built about 1845. Star Junction buildings and structures were also comprised of 22 mine manager's homes, located on, "Tony Row," and two former mine buildings, two churches, a parsonage, two commercial buildings, a concrete highway bridge, built in 1921, and an earthen dam reservoir established in 1892.

Notable people from Star Junction, Tim Litvin, country singer, who has released four albums, most recently "The Reason."

I would love to say that the paranormal encounters ended in Star Junction, but they have only gotten worse. Instead of fearing them, we have learned to embrace them. Our friends and family have witnessed many of these supernatural events with us and although it scares several of them, they understand that some things are beyond our control and totally inescapable. It has become apparent to us that the ghosts have a story to tell.

The stories that I am sharing with you are real. We have lived them. We to this day have no clue as to why we have experienced so many paranormal encounters, but we feel fortunate that we have. We seek them out only after the ghosts tag us first. I am a novice writer who wishes to share with those who question the unexplained. If you ask our opinion, we will tell you without a doubt that the ghosts are real.

Sherri, her husband, John, and their three daughters have traveled the United States extensively in search of haunted properties and venues. Sherri and John both grew up in ghost-infested houses. Sherri once lived in a morgue turned basement apartment in Klamath Falls, Oregon when she was eight. John grew up in Pennsylvania in a house that never slept due to the, "round the clock" activity that frequently occurred from ornery ghosts and poltergeists.

Instead of fearing the paranormal, they decided to embrace, investigate and understand it. Their goal is to seek out the hundreds of locations that exhibit the combination of history, paranormal and unexplained circumstances that draw people in from all over the world. Sherri and her family currently live in Allegheny County, Pennsylvania.

Klamath Falls, Oregon, 1972 Through 1977: I too lived in several haunted properties, and for whatever reason, we always seemed to live near cemeteries. I live in two different homes as a child that sat next to one of Oregons most haunted graveyards. The Linkville cemetery, located in Klamath Falls ran across my backyard when I lived on Johnston Street, and later it was just a block away when I lived on N. 11th Street. I never gave much thought about the cemetery when I was a kid, in fact I used it as a short-cut enroute to Fairview Elementary. It was later in life that I learned that it fell on several lists where ghost sightings and other supernatural circumstances have been witnessed.

For a brief time we lived on Esplanade in the morgue section of the Blackburn Sanitarium. The building was also once used as a hospital, but was later turned into apartments. I was only eight, but I can remember that the apartment always felt chilly and dark despite the fact that it was the end of summer, and it always felt like someone was watching me.

Noises, possibly from the ancient steam heaters kept me awake throughout the night, and I often woke up to the air in the room feeling oddly heavy. With that heaviness came an indescribable odor that permeated the room reminiscent of burning matches.

Discussing these strange events with anyone would have been unheard of considering that paranormal activity was in its infancy as far as media hype and ghost shows were concerned, but my grandparents had often spoke of ghosts. We had previously lived in a haunted plantation house in Middletown, Delaware during the late sixties, so I knew a little bit about the walking dead, but not enough that I was comfortable living in the same space with them.

As a child with a vivid and extreme imagination, my suspicions of us living in the same quarters with ghosts were confirmed when I overheard my mother talking to the next door neighbor, Julie concerning just how creepy the whole building was. Julie swore that she had seen a dark entity walking through her bedroom and then she just disappeared through a wall. Soon after that I had my own experience in the building sometime during the early winter one day when I was bored and decided to explore the building.

I entered the building through the main front doors, and then I headed for the forbidden upstairs area. Looking down as I counted the steps, I immediately walked head on, straight into a man who was coming down the main steps located in the hallway leading from the upstairs apartments into the main foyer. I remember saying sorry, but my words were spoken to thin air because there was absolutely nobody there when I looked up. That image has never left my mind.

It was just too vivid to ignore, and it was all too real to not look back on it as paranormal. Not long after my incident with the ghost man, our neighbor Julie moved out of her apartment into a new home, and shortly after her departure, we moved to the other side of town, to Johnson Street, right next to the most haunted cemetery in Oregon. The Linkville Cemetery opened me up to a whole new world of discovery for the one short year that we lived there.

It is no secret that many of the sanitariums of the late eighteen hundreds through the mid nineteen hundreds had a reputation for treating mentally ill patients and those with deadly diseases and other unfavorable conditions in a way that was anything but humane.

Questionable patient management now reviewed as barbaric ranged from total isolation with months without actual human contact to cold water or shock treatments to rib removal which was thought to allow the lungs to expand. At the time they were considered to be top rate medical practices that often left patients fearing for their lives.

Renovations to the historical building beautified the interior, but it did nothing to quiet the inner turmoil they lay dormant inside the red brick exterior of the once very active sanitarium. Ghosts, dark shadows, spirits, orbs, voices, electrical problems, static on the phone lines and strange odors were constant complaints from those who lived or worked at the building for the last 70 years. Frat parties managed to drum up the most paranormal activity, perhaps due to the extreme noise that disturbed the spirits during a time of rest.

Students reportedly moved out just as fast as they moved in, and the rumor mill has it down that is was due to the multiple sightings of ghosts walking up the steps that simply vanished into thin air, and the faint sound of whispering that echoed through the halls all hours of the night keeping them from their studies. Dark shadows are always reportedly lurking in the basement and far away voices are forever coming from somewhere deep underneath the building. They are nothing short of disturbing to those that have heard them.

Many believe that the frequent renovations on the building have stirred up the tormented people who were once housed here, and this has become even more apparent to those that have witnessed the many ghosts that appear to those that cannot ignore their sickly frame as being desperate souls who are wearing nothing more then a thin hospital gown and carrying a look of grave illness that passed with them into death.

The entire building possesses the feel of heaviness and is often cold despite warm weather or other sources of heat. The basement that once housed deceased patients is now apartments. This was once our home and the start of my raw glimpse into the paranormal.

The Romanesque style apartment building at 1842 Esplanade is hard to ignore when you take in its grand stance that is evident of antiquated elegance hidden behind years of sadness and decay. The Blackburn Sanitarium now goes by the name of Blackburn Manor and has been placed on the National Register of Historic Places. It is now privately owned.

Again, the subject of paranormal activity and talking about ghosts in many situations is taboo due to the obvious. People either think that you are crazy, have a chemical inbalance or that you have a seriously flawed imagination. I once agreed with this until I started to recount the many unexplained events that took place during my childhood.

Tonopah, Nevada 1984: The town of Tonopah is located halfway between Las Vegas and Reno, Nevada. The silver and gold boom of the early1900's quickly breathed life into the small community. The Mizpah Hotel opened to the public in 1907 to accommodate the miners. According to the thousands of visitors who have stayed at the famously haunted Mizpah Hotel over the years, it is not uncommon to see a ghost miner or the spirit of the lady in red.

There is nothing particularly scary about an old miner walking around a specific premise; that is unless he has been deceased for 70 years, and he is in your hotel room opening and closing the window all night.

According to the thousands of visitors who have stayed at the famously haunted Mizpah Hotel over the years, this is in no way an abnormal event. In fact most of these guests have come to expect ghostly anomalies and highly spirited apparitions that surround the historic hotel and many have come to enjoy the eerie atmosphere that encompasses the historic stone and brick building.

The Mizpah Hotel opened their doors to the public in 1907 to accommodate the miners and anyone else who needed a hot meal or soft feathered bed to sleep off a day's hard work. Billed as the most impressive hotel from San Francisco to Denver, and rightfully so as the Mizpah left no stone unturned when it came to the best of the best for their guests.

The grand hotel offered electric lights, steam heat, artfully crafted ceiling fans in each room, an elegant dining room, and fully stocked bar with the best whiskey on the planet, and a full scale casino that was like no other in its time.

Once word spread, miners weren't the only guests of the five-story Victorian-style hotel that put Tonopah on the map. High stakes gamblers, highfalutin businessmen and other weary travelers sore from the rough rides of the stagecoaches and early Ford motor cars often stopped in for a meal, a chance at lady luck, and a night's rest.

Female workers were also a large part of the energized atmosphere at the Mizpah Hotel. Despite the times, prostitutes were capable of being self reliant due to earnings from working by tending to the miner's needs after a hard day of picking away at the gold and silver veins. These women were tough, but the busy hotel allowed for them to live a life of relative ease.

It is believed that a few of the prostitutes still walk the halls of the hotel in search of work still today. The Lady in Red is a highly active ghost, and is spotted the most by visitors. Men often report that she has touched their hair or they feel slight tingles from where she has brushed against them.

Her perfume wafting through the hotel is undeniable, and she is sometimes seen talking to an old miner. It is believed that the Lady in Red was murdered by a jealous boyfriend who beat her and then strangled her after she exited a room on the sixth floor of the hotel.

Another apparition that has been seen by only a few visitors and paranormal investigators appears to the human eye as a woman, but hazy and greenish blue. She vanishes just as fast as you catch sight of her.

Several older men have been seen walking throughout the hotel, but they disappear through walls and thin air. A few of these ghosts are dressed in their best finery. Other more down to earth ghosts are obviously gold and silver miners if you judge their category by their clothing. A few active spirits that wish to be seen will appear at the foot of the beds where guests are sleeping.

Back in its heyday, before the Mizpah fell into a state of shambles I had the pleasure of dining at the restaurant before it closed its doors in early 2000. The ghost stories were part of the conversation at almost every table as everyone waited in hopes of spotting the Lady in Red.

Unfortunately we witnessed nothing, but the staff informed us that she normally came out at night, and we were still several hours away from darkness. Sadly, the empty building lost the previous luster that it once embodied due to a lack of patrons and care.

The new owners Fred and Nancy Cline plan to bring life back to the Mizpah, and that includes a casino, bar, hotel, restaurant, a full staff, and several ghostly guests that will entertain guests in the event that boredom strikes while staying at the historic hotel.

If history repeats itself, no bathtub will be safe at the Mizpah Hotel, at least not from an elected official who has been deceased for many decades, but remains highly spirited, especially when there is a bathroom involved. According to records the politician died in the hotel on the night of a Nevada state election.

Attempting to hide his death, his aides kept his body on blocks of ice in a bathtub while waiting until after he'd won re-election before making the announcement that he would not be holding office due to his most recent quieted state of being. Prior to the hotel closing in 2000, guests could almost expect to see the politician laughing near one of the bathtubs found in the fifty-room hotel.

The typical basement is creepy in any situation, but at the Mizpah Hotel you can add in a total fear fest of highly eerie and creepy circumstances right down to the 11-year-old dirty laundry that remains in a giant heap where it was left when the hotel closed down in 2000.

Dark corners filled with cobwebs add to the creepiness, as does the replica of an old mine-shaft, once used to entertain guests. Apparitions of miners are a regular occurrence in the extremely large basement, but if you try to follow them they will walk right through a wall to remove themselves from your peering eyes.

Tonopah, Nevada can with no doubt be added onto the list as being a big part of the Wild West, and the Mizpah Hotel had its share of wild and ruddy guests. One legend has it that Wyatt Earp and Jack Dempsey once worked at the hotel, but no supporting evidence has shown this to be a fact. However there are two rooms at the hotel that features these two legends names.

Location: Main Street and Brougher Avenue, Tonopah, Nevada.

Belle Vernon, Pennsylvania, 1990: We had just moved back to Pennsylvania after living in California for a short time. I was pregnant, and John had found a job that required him to work a lot of hours. We found a house on 1st Street, located next to the Christian Church on Main Street, near the Belle vernon Volunteer Fire Department.

The two-story rental had an eerie feel to it from the start. At the time, we had Collie that was afraid of the cellar, and I had two young daughters who were constantly complaining that they were scared to be upstairs at night. Because of this fear, our oldest daughter, Jennifer decided that she would sleep on the couch one night and wait for her dad to get home from work.

She was awaken sometime during the night and found a ghost man standing next to the couch. He was wearing a plaid shirt. Her screaming woke me up, but by the time that I made my way downstairs, the ghost was gone. The house became something straight out of a horror movie scene after that night.

Dishes would fly out of the dish strainer. Objects would sway back and forth on the walls, and you would here footsteps running up and down the steps. We would arrive home after a day out, only to find our mattresses flipped and hanging halfway off of the bed. Things would be moved or completely disappear, but would resurface at a later date. On many different ocassions, our friends and family would question the things that we all witnessed in the house during get togethers, but we never really had an explanation as to who or what was making the home so unlivable.

Friends began to stay with me and the girls while John worked at night. The house never slept despite how many people were there. It was constant chaos filled with disembodied footsteps and the feeling of always being watched. I prepared a nursery for our new baby that soon became the focal point of the ghosts attention. Once I delivered our third daughter, Joni, we would find her at the other side of the crib from where I had layed her down originally. A few times, we left her in her baby carrier next to our bed, but the kids would let us know that the carrier was at the top of the steps on the landing.

Our middle daughter, Jessica was pushed down the steps by an entity when she was two. Luckily we were able to catch her and break the fall. We questioned the neighbors about the house and was informed that a boy had fallen out of an upstairs window and that a coal miner had died of a heart attack in the upstairs hallway.

They then told us that the house had a negative history of various tales involving ghosts and that nobody stayed long in the house. Soon after that conversation, we were woke up to the smell of fire coming from our livingroom. Once downstairs we discovered that our lamp had caught fire. That month we decided it was time to move.

Yuma, Arizona 1991: Shortly after the birth of our third daughter, Joni, we moved from Belle Vernon, Pennsylvania back to the west coast to be near my parents who lived in Yuma, Arizona. We rented a townhouse that showed no indication of supernatural activity, but given our history of dealing with the paranormal, this was a short lived notion.

We received a break on the deposit provided that I clean the townhouse before moving in. It was a beautiful property despite the one hideous feature...the brown stove in the kitchen that stuck out like a misshappen and ugly object that made my eyes instantly bleed. I tackled oven's filth with a vengeance. All was going well until my wet, dirty rag hit on the blackest spot that lay deep with the beast.

Once I hit the bullseye on my target, I was promptly shot across the room. I was immediately met with a severe pain that rocketed up my arm. My husband came running to me after he heard my screams. After investigating the reason for my attack, he informed me that I had been electrocuted by an empty light socket that held a charge of 220. I was lucky to be alive.

This incident was followed by things that to this day I do not understand. Clearing my head, I walked into the adjacent living space where the second floor steps descended into the livingroom. It was here that I witnessed a glowing orb of sorts that began bouncing down the steps, forming into a full apparition of a person that dissipated literally in front of my eyes just as fast as it had manifested.

Crest Avenue, Charleroi, PA. 1992: This one rental house that should never have even crossed our radar, but the price was right for our meager income, so we signed a one year lease that led us straight into the depths of hell. Right after entering the gate, we experienced unexplained phenomenon. The house emanated a smell similar to sulfur that penetrated out of the basement. We were continuely woke up in the middle of the night from the sensation that something was touching you, and then the the smell of smoke would alarm you in to thinking that the house was on fire.

Objects in our home were continually misplaced, the kids started seeing shadows in the hallway, and I experienced an apparition floating above my head one night after being awaken in bed from a nightmare. I immediately noticed that there was a form above me. I was too scared to scream, and just as fast as the ghost appeared, it was gone. That image is etched in my mind forever.

Our youngest daughter, Joni was only two years old at the time that we lived in the rental. She was experiencing the sight of a white form that manifested into the spirit of a woman. It happened once while she was playing upstairs in their bedroom, and once in the hallway. We could hear her talking to someone, so I went up to investigate what was happening to our toddler. Upon entering their bedroom, I too witnessed the ghost lady.

She disappeared immediately, but not before I had taken in her full form. I ran out of the bedroom and flew down our stairway in what felt like one continous step. I almost broke my leg from the traumatic jump. We moved shortly after the blizzard of 1993 back to the west coast. To this day, we all clearly remember that paranormal encounter.

Bodie, California Ghost Town 1996: After visiting Bodie, we had a year of extreme bad luck. After attempting to figure out why our world had changed so drastically, we learned that our youngest daughter had taken a souvenir from the haunted ghost town despite warnings posted at Bodie, informing you of pending "bad luck" for taking anything that you may find lying around while on your tour. After talking with our girls, we quickly realized why we had met with several disasters in last last several months. Once we became informed, we sent the souvenir back to Bodie with an apology. Amazingly, the bad luck stopped almost immediately.

The Curse of Bodie: Visitors are warned that everything in Bodie ghost town is a part of the historic scene and is fully protected, and that nothing is allowed to be collected or removed from the park. According to many letters from past visitors displayed throughout the Bodie Museum, the consequences of taking so much as a rusty nail from the dirt streets of Bodie ghost town has led to a curse that includes illnesses, bad luck, and accidents from non-believing guests that have taken the souvenirs home.

These same visitors promptly returned their souvenirs, along with apologetic letters to the ghost town without hesitation or question. Some people truly believe in the curse while others shrug it off as mere superstition. You will have to decide for yourself.

The Lawless and Gun Slinging Ghosts of the West: Waterman S. Body, also known as William S. Bodey first discovered gold in Bodie, California around 1859, but the larger discovery of several rich gold veins in 1876 couldn't be kept a secret for long as they were worth $75 million. The news spread like wild fire which quickly started a frenzy of greedy miners on a mad dash to Bodie to claim their fair share. Long days of mining, hot temperatures, and flaring tempers brought the need for relaxing, gambling, and down time.

Alcohol was in high demand, and the under paid Chinese railroad workers made sure that the town was well stocked with it or they would suffer the consequences. Bodie's name would have been better suited as "Party Town" as there were 65 saloons lining the one mile main street and seven breweries running around the clock with whiskey being brought in by 100 gallon barrels at a time in horse drawn carriages. Killings were a daily activity, and bank robberies, stagecoach hold-ups, along with street fighting was a common activity among the people of Bodie.

The town had a reputation of being one of the most furious, vehement, violent and lawless towns in all the Mother Lode. Most fights were fueled by alcohol consumption, greed, and jealousy surrounding the ladies in the red light district. It was not uncommon for fights to end by a bullet being put into someone by the day's end as this was their way of settling an argument. The fire bell rang often and long as it was used to count the rapidly growing deceased residents along with their age at the time of burial. On September 5, 1880, the daily Bodie Standard reported three shootings and two holdups of stages in one single day.

Bodie only had a brief period of glory, lasting from 1879 to 1882, however the decline was slow as the Bodie and Standard mines merged in 1887 and operated successfully for the next two decades. In 1892 a disastrous fire struck, with another fire following in 1932, destroying much of the town, and a further decline of residents in Bodie resulted from prohibition and the Depression, but some mining continued.

By the 1950s Bodie became a ghost town as residents no longer had a reason to stay, and with no moving companies in the town of Bodie, the remaining residents simply packed what they could on one wagon or truck and left the rest behind. Many of Bodies buildings still contain belongings that were left here from years ago, and can be seen in the houses and businesses that still stands in the ghost town.

The gold mining ghost town of Bodie is located in the eastern slopes of the Sierra, close to the Nevada border, and once boasted a population of 10,000 people as gold seekers flocked to the town to get rich quick. Today only about 150 of the original buildings remain, but there is just enough of them left to give you a solid feeling of the way things once were in this wild town. Bodie is a very unique ghost town as it has the largest number of standing structures left in a state of untouched arrested decay.

Bodie is watched over by dedicated workers of the California State Park system who have made it their duty to ensure that Bodie remains as close to its original state as possible. Because of the extreme care, historic detail and attention to Bodie ghost town, history buffs can briefly go back in time when viewing the remaining structures and cemetery filled by very young deceased residents, easily allowing visitors to imagine what life was like in this boom-town by exploring the streets. Thankfully time has been kind to this popular ghost town, leaving it looking pretty much the same as it did in 1880.

Linesville, Pennsylvania: The historic Knickerbocker Hotel has a long reputation for being haunted. Guests are often fooled by the hotel's tranquil appearance of peaceful calm as it sits nestled on an unassuming street corner, located in the borough of Linesville, Pennsylvania. In most storms though, the calm usually buffers the signs of what is to come once all hell breaks loose, and once you have stepped foot in the Knickerbocker's front door, you will discover why it is a well-known hotbed of paranormal commotion at it's best.

Since the early 1900s reports to the hotel owners have flooded in concerning objects being moved and thrown across the room by unseen forces. Several guests claim to have been touched by what can only be explained as the sensation of cold fingers, and a few have had the sensation of being pulled, pushed or shoved while on the staircase. Chilling sounds later played back from electronic voice phenomena recordings conducted over the last decade can only be interpreted as spirit voices since there was nobody in the room and they were recorded in complete silence at different times by Keystone Paranormal, Paranormal State and the Oil Region Paranormal Investigation Team.

Built in 1882 by M.A. Arnold, the Knickerbocker Hotel was originally owned and ran by the Arnold family. The family lived in the upper part of the hotel. Sadness and loss quickly found it's way to the Arnold family with the death of Clara Arnold, who succumbed to tuberculosis, just three years after the hotel was built. Clara Arnold was just 37 years old when her life ended so dramatically on that cold, wintry day in February of 1885.

It is believed that she more than likely died in her own bed in the hotel where the family resided in the living quarters. The grave plot records from the Linesville Cemetery indicate that the family lost a young child some time before Clara Arnold passed away.

The headstone of Clara and her child are located at the eastern end of the cemetery, just off of Wallace Avenue, less than a mile from the hotel in row 44; graves 4 & 5. The remaining four Arnold family plots today set empty. Today, Clara's ghost and the spirit of her young child are strong presences at the Knickerbocker. A tiny tot has been heard laughing and giggling despite there being no children staying at the establishment at the time of the reported incident.

Since 2005, Peg and Myrle Knickerbocker have owned the haunted hotel. The couple were aware of the many ghost stories that have circulated around the Crawford County business for more than one-hundred years. None of this bothered the open-minded couple, but of course Peg is a Sensitive who has the ability to pick up on vibrations that make her susceptible to external agents and minute differences within the surrounding energy and atmosphere.

On her own, Peg has captured footage of ectoplasmic mist that she has posted on the investigations page of their website. Guests and several investigative groups have been presented with similar evidence while staying at the hotel.

While visiting the Knickerbocker Hotel, ORPIT had the experience of capturing an unexplained black mass encompassing a nearby rocking chair during their investigation. The anomaly did not appear in the shape of a person or apparition, but instead came across as a unified body of matter with no specific definition. The owners will openly tell you that some people hear voices at the Knickerbocker, while others see things. Not many enter the front door without feeling something that is undeniably chilling. To date, all of the psychic and mediums who have been to the haunted establishment have had at least one of these experiences.

Location: 115 W. Erie Street, Linesville, Pennsylvania.

Tonoaph, Nevada

Summer of 2013, Livermore, Pennsylvania: Our group was searching for a great location to search for ghosts due to our recent purchase of ghost hunting equipment. After receiving a few tips, we headed out to the West Penn Trail, located in Indiana County, PA. We had our sights set on the small town of Livermore since it had been dubbed, "sunken & haunted." We parked in the common area and headed out for the trail that led us to a bridge that offered views of Livermore and what was left of it. Above the bridge, just beyond a trail that traveled through a thick foliaged hill, we located the old cemetery.

We explored the entire grounds from below the bride, the cemetery and onward down the path to unknown perimeters. The eerie sounds never stopped. As we spoke of the many legends surrounding the town that included a ghost lady who appeared to be dressed in black garb. She was always spotted pushing a baby carriage across the bridge, and while we never met up with her, our group of twelve met up with a strange mist that encompassed us just above our heads in the shape of arms reaching out with long finges that appeared to be trying to pull us in. Needless to say, we all ran back to the car as fast as our legs would move.

Lurking just beyond highway 22 in the heart of Pennsylvania, down a long country road, inhabits a few dark and mysterious creatures that will put a certain fear into the strongest of men once they dare to come face to face with them. It is not any one particular entity that can be seen by the human eye, although a few lay claims to having witnessed their terrifying form; but they can definitely be felt on just about any given night by the many of us who sense that uncanny fear for the unnatural things that exist within our universe.

If this hasn't gotten your attention then maybe a few restless corpses, wandering apparitions, sunken buildings and an angry dead witch will do the trick. This is only some of what you will find when you visit the diminished under-water town of Livermore, Pennsylvania. Once a booming community during the 1800's, flooding by the Flood Control Act of the United States Congress permanently silenced the community forever, or so they thought.

Livermore, Pennsylvania was established in 1827 and grew slightly once a railroad and canal were firmly put into place. Some of the local legends has it that a witch was drawn to the beauty of the area and eventually made the town her home, enchanting the residents with her powers. However not all of the good people were bewitched by her spells, and it has been said that the towns people burned her to death, and she cursed the town to damaging floods while her flesh burned into that of a corpse.

Unfortunately the witches curse was coming into play as a severe flood on the anniversary of her death in 1889 permanently closed the bustling canal that once allowed travel from Johnstown to Pittsburgh along with connections to nearby Blairsville and Saltsburg. In 1936 Livermore once again succumbed to flood waters, submerging the buildings and residents to flood waters reaching 18 feet.

The great St. Patrick's Day flood was the towns beginning of the end of Livermore as structural damages to the small town was much too severe to fully recuperate its former status. One resident died from the flood and $500 million in damages was more then the town could handle. The Flood Control Acts of 1936 and 1938 left Livermore with a future of being fully submerged underwater forever.

Visitors to Livermore claim that you can see images of the structures that once stood mirrored on the surface of the water, and when the water levels get low you can see roof tops and chimneys of the homes that once made Livermore a town. Screeching noises from no apparent source, distinct howling noises, dark images, ghostly figures, red eyes, and a foul smell that will leave your hair standing on end are only some of the reports that people have stated feeling, seeing or smelling in the past. The cemetery is another story within itself. The feeling of being followed and watched never leaves you through your whole visit to the resting place of the damned.

The old Livermore Cemetery now rests on top of the hill above the sunken town where the deceased once lived. It was a requirement by the Flooding Act that it be moved due to contamination of disturbing buried coffins by means of purposely flooding the area. However the legend tells us that the cemetery was moved so that the dead could rest below the dirt instead of water. You will find the haunted graveyard at the end of Livermore road, which also happens to be the entrance to the West Penn Trail.

The Livermore Cemetery sign is still intact and it is the original that was used in the black and white version of Night of the Living Dead, the actual movie itself was filmed an hour away in Evans City, Pennsylvania. Some of the hot spots in Livermore include dated bridges, with the most popular being at the beginning of the West Penn trail. Once you have passed the gate, make a left and at this bridge your fate awaits you in the form of fear.

When visiting Livermore make sure to proceed with caution as police do patrol the area. Respect the graves of the deceased or they will haunt you forever. Take a camera, flashlight, extra batteries, and quite possibly some extra underwear "just in case".

Livermore is also known as Satan's Seat due to the complex nature of the repeated floods that never allowed the town to replenish itself into a healthy form, but rather it remained contaminated by murky waters that continually kept it lurking into the depths of a damned dampened darkness, and eventually ruins and death.

Livermore, PA. Is located 40 miles east of Pittsburgh. Take I-376 E to Highway 22/E. William Penn Highway. Turn left on Livermore Road and continue straight.

I have written about hundreds of haunted locations, but we have only been to half of those that I have written about. Many people write to me, asking that I share their experiences with ghosts. To date, we continue to experience encounters with the paranormal, but the ones that matter to us most are the hardest to connect with. The ghost sightings have become ridiculous in nature and count, but in an attempt to share with the puclic our experiences, here are a few of the places that we have traveled to and found proof that the ghosts are real....

The Ghost of Edgar Allan Poe: We have visited the Westminster Burial Grounds twice, but found nothing but a peaceful setting except for the homeless that sit around waiting for handouts. Despite the eerie calm, this graveyard is considered to be one of the most haunted cemeteries in the United States. Just a few blocks away, Edgar's house awaits your visit in what is now a museum. It is also a quiet place, but you cannot help but to image that he is watching over your shoulder at every turn.

It is occupied with famous and restless walking corpses from generals and mayors to influential businessmen and writers. One of those famous writers, often referred to as the dark poet aka Edgar Allan Poe, refuses to believe that he is dead and makes every attempt to demonstrate this by showing up on his birthday every year since his death in 1849.

Once you step foot into the ethereal and antiquated cemetery, there is absolutely no question that you have just wandered into a place where nothing living could possibly exist in a natural state. You also realize that the forbidden eeriness of the dark shadows lurking about instantly chill your bones and the raunchy stench remotely resembles that of a rotting corpse.

It has been considered one of the most haunted cemeteries in the United States due to the high amount of paranormal activity witnessed by people simply walking past it. Depending on whom you are and your thought process over haunted destinations and active dark spirits, the Western Burial Ground of the Westminster Presbyterian Church yard in Baltimore,

Maryland could be considered one of the best cemeteries to visit or it could be on your list of worst nightmare vacation destinations.

Dark legends filled with shocking truths have permanently scarred the Westminster Presbyterian Western Burial Ground in Baltimore, Maryland since it was originally constructed in 1786. The church was built directly over the burial grounds, and finally completed in 1852, but the structures original massive arches created underground catacombs that have been a constant source of supernatural occurrences and other unexplained phenomena, both below and above ground.

Over time bodies were constantly disarranged and even removed from their original resting place in an effort to accommodate the strict policies that city officials once enforced in the mid 1800's. Medical students also took part in these disturbances as dissecting bodies was a common practice in gaining medical knowledge. Soldiers from the civil war took refuge within the catacombs and stored weapons and other gear within the tombs.

Safety and health concerns that loomed within Baltimore's city limits soon became apparent, and cemeteries were to be accompanied by a church. This posed a slight problem as the burial grounds already existed. Underground pathways ran amuck underneath the busy city streets, but these passageways were often times the only access to buried loved ones.

If visiting with the young ghost of forty year-old Edgar Allan Poe intrigues you, then this is the place to be in the middle of winter. He has been spotted on various accounts, but most sightings are around his birth date of January 19th. The Raven is completely dressed in a black wool waistcoat and trousers, donning a wide brimmed black hat, and a dark scarf wrapped around his face, possibly to hide it from the view of curious gawkers. His solid cat's head walking stick can be heard tapping against the hard ground of the earth as he strolls through the cemetery.

Ghostly tales that have sustained surround the fact that many of these restless souls wandering the burial grounds were buried in the cemetery alive. Once they passed over to the spiritual side, their spirit began to wander the grounds while seeking out the person or group of people that buried them alive in order to get revenge for putting them through such a savage death. There are quite a few unsettled spirits at this haunted graveyard who seem to be forever looking for something that they just cannot find, and they often frighten the individuals that stumble upon them during their search.

Many paranormal experts believe that the problem exists within the original construction and lay-out of the burial grounds and the church. Not all of the deceased can be properly visited due to bad planning. Some of the headstones are unreadable due to their age, and visitors to the cemetery are unaware of the hard to find parts of the graveyard that have been partially covered by the massive Gothic Revival- style Westminster Church. The hidden underground catacombs are the only access to some of the most restless souls on the planet.

Muffled screams from a seemingly bottomless dark pit from an unknown destination found deep below the earth can be heard and compared to as a personal human hell simply from the depth of the anguish felt by the living when hearing their tortured screams. Ghosts and restless spirits aimlessly roam the dark underground passageways of the catacombs that are encompassed by a foul stench, and a white haired entity is often seen walking slowly through the grave markers in apparent search of something.

Rumors, legends and ghost stories have remained a part of the cemeteries rich history due to actual communication and ghost sightings by living beings visiting the burial grounds. Amateur ghost hunters, paranormal investigators, physics and thrill seekers quite often experience paranormal activity by talking and communicating almost telepathically with those who have crossed over and are now part of the spirit world just by visiting the massive grounds that holds them prisoner. These lonely spirits appear to be anxious to tell their story and visit with the living souls that may finally accomplish putting them to rest at last.

The Western Burial Ground of the Westminster Presbyterian Church yard in Baltimore, Maryland has had its share of paranormal investigators, but there is no doubt that Edgar Allan Poe's birthday is by far one of the hottest peaks for communicating with the dead. Curator Jeff Jerome invited 70 guests and one photographer to gather at the grave site of the famous poet on his birthday. They celebrated by reading his works, and drank dark amontillado sherry to emulate a featured drink from one of Poe's many horror stories.

The photographer waited patiently for the moment that a ghostly encounter would occur, and before he could say cheese, the entire group witnessed the spirit of a light haired man dressed in black running through the cemetery carrying a cane. He kneeled down at the poet's grave; then quietly vanished into the dark night air. They later reported that the ghost wore a period frock coat, and they found that flowers had been placed on his grave. Life magazine featured the haunting picture that was captured by infrared night-vision equipment, and the experts deemed the photo of the entity as a real spirit.

Several other encounters with ghosts have been reported by ghost hunters and paranormal investigators looking for proof that the dead walk among us, but many visitors of the burial grounds are there to pay their respects. It would appear however that the spirit world has repugnance for living souls as they are often taunted by the spirits living there. The casualties of war included Generals Samuel Smith and John Stricker, who were both laid to rest at the Westminster Presbyterian Western Burial Ground.

Lucia Watson Taylor: Sixteen year old Lucia Watson Taylor is a frequent visitor of the cemetery, especially if it is dark and misty. Her white flowing dress is hard to miss, as is her beautiful head of long hair. The problem with this vision is that she crossed over in late 1816, but she has been seen praying within the burial grounds on many an occasion. Dark figures, hazy spirits, ghostly sightings, footsteps, screams, laughing, and indescribable rancid odors are all a part of these older then dirt resting grounds that never rests.

Over time bodies have been disturbed from their original resting place in an effort to accommodate the strict policies that city officials once enforced in the mid 1800's. Safety and health concerns that loomed within Baltimore's city limits soon became apparent, and cemeteries were to be accompanied by a church. This posed a slight problem as the burial grounds already existed.

The grandfather of President James Buchanan attempts to rest in the confines of this highly spirited playground for ghosts, and several unsavory spirits roam the grounds in an effort to chase off disrespectful thrill seekers that refuse to keep the noise at a level that allows the spirits to sleep. Generals, soldiers, statesmen, politicians and crazed lunatic, Leona Wellesley are all buried deep within the deep rich soils of the 18th-century style burial grounds; however they have undoubtedly left the confines of their wooden boxes that housed them upon final viewing, and are now walking among the many visitors that have come to see them.

A letter by Edgar Allan Poe to Frederick W. Thomas, written on February 14, 1849, states: Depend upon it, after all, Thomas, Literature is the most noble of professions. In fact, it is about the only one fit for a man. For my own part, there is no seducing me from the path."

Location: 519 West Fayette Street, Baltimore, Maryland. The cemetery is open to the public.

Avella, Pennsylvania: Welcome to Avella, Pennsylvania, established during the mid 1800s by frontiersmen and farmers, and eventually put on the map by coal miners and railroad workers. Avella is merely a ghost town located on the outskirts of the plush interior of Washington County, Pennsylvania, and bordering with Brooke County, West Virginia. It is known for beautiful scenery and a multitude of wildlife, including several species of birds.

There is another side to Avella that is dark, diabolical and recognized for being actively haunted by the coal miners that once rioted a nearby non-union coal mine in 1922 that ended with devastating results. Eight miners and Brooke County Sheriff, H.H. Duval lost their lives that fateful day, several other miners were confirmed dead, and placed in unmarked graves along the wooded area now known as the Shades of Death Road.

European immigrants flocked to southwestern Pennsylvania to work in the coal mines that offered less than cozy conditions, but guaranteed pay and food on the table. The days were long and hard, and the money kept the men and their families barely above the poverty level during the late 1800s and into the early 1900s. The winters were brutal and the work was monotonous as work began at daybreak and ended at sundown.

Coal mining was a hard life for the miners and their families, and their lives were often shortened due to brutal circumstances sustained by work injuries from tools, cave-ins and explosions from dynamite that was faulty or quite often miscalculated. Many of these men suffered from a loss of limbs, suffocation, third degree burns, and wounds that quickly became infected. The screams of the wounded miners were unmistakable, and could be heard by the wives and children awaiting their arrival home after a long day at work.

The Shades of Death Road has long been a mystery to the locals, as well as the many unsuspecting people that have traveled along the deep country road and have heard the eerie noises that mimic blood curdling screams, cries of anguish and even growling. Unexplained anomalies are no stranger to this hauntingly mysterious road, and it is quite likely that you will be privy to ghosts that have missing limbs and burned or damaged extremities.

This whole stretch of road has had its share of dead people becoming part of the dense scenery, but they are not where you can see them, they are hidden deep under the rich soil of long ago, forgotten and in unmarked graves. You can however see them when they decide to appear at different times during the day and night, calling out to whoever is willing to listen to their cries of help. Driver distractions could explain the hundreds of automobile accidents that have taken place on this haunted stretch of tree lined roadway.

The reports from crash survivors are all basically the same. A dark figured darted across the road in front of their vehicle or they witnessed a glowing white apparition that appeared to be in distress, and vanished into thin air. Both sightings have caused a multitude of drivers to crash into one of the many trees lining both sides of the road.

The local legend firmly holds onto the possibility that the Shades of Death Road is in fact haunted due to a large amount of lives lost through unexpected mining accidents, and the road was at one time heavily occupied from dawn to dusk. Other local folklore includes the story of an escaped slave that was hung from a tree overhanging the road, and when you consider that most of the road is one long brilliant tunnel of trees, the mere thought of his ghost walking along the road, touching those that dare to come in for a closer look, well it just doesn't get any creepier then that.

Pittsburgh, PA to Shades of Death Road in Avella, PA: Take Steubenville Pike, Bavington Rd, PA-18 S, Langeloth Road and Bethel Ridge Road to Shades of Death Rd in Avella.

Directions to Shades of Death Road from the center of Avella, Pennsylvania, approximately 8 miles: Start out going Northwest on Avella Road/PA-50 West toward Cross Creek Road. Turn left on Cross Creek Road. Turn left onto Paris Road. Turn right onto Campbell Drive. Turn left onto the Shades of Death Road.

Route 666: Route 666, the 193 mile highway to hell that has often been referred to as a "beast of a highway" or "the Devil's highway" due to the significance of the triple digit number, the many lives that have been lost along its unforgiving stretch of asphalt, and the high amount of reported paranormal activity. After years of complaints and debating, the American Association of State Highway and Transportation Officials assigned a new set of highway digits for the U.S. state route that runs through Utah, Arizona, Colorado, and New Mexico.

The complex system devised of a numbering plan made up by the Joint Board on Interstate Highways had many components, but with an easy to understand system comprised of even numbers for roads running east to west and odd numbers for roads running north to south.

Highway 491 has taken the place of route 666 beginning in Gallup, New Mexico with old highway markers still standing in place as reminders as to what once was. However the original numbers take precedence over any new numbers and can't even begin to disguise the ugly truth that remains when it comes to the large amount of ghost sightings and other unexplained paranormal activity that seems to cause destruction along its path. Highway 491 continues north through Colorado and Utah and ends at the intersection of U.S. 191 in Monticello, Utah.

Route 666 has a long history that stems from its beginning in 1926 due to it being the sixth branch of what is now the defunct Route 66, and therefore became the infamous Route 666, and had virtually nothing to do with Lucifer as far as the numbering system was concerned. Most of the beast of a highway is now been renamed to Highway 191 which runs north to south. Running east to west is the historic route 66 that runs across the central part of New Mexico and is now known as route 40.

Unexplained mysteries attached to highway 666 are hard to ignore when you view the statistics associated with this now renamed highway. The amount of accidents is insurmountable, the paranormal incidences are too many to ignore and the so-called bad luck along this stretch of road has lead to state highway officials being pummeled with requests from all four states to change the name of the highway so that mishaps, deaths and other unexplained phenomena can finally be put to rest.

After all there is nothing creepier than driving late at night on a deserted road that has aptly been named after the antichrist, and delivers a sideshow of strange events almost nightly. Reports of ghost hitchhikers walking along the darkened highway and strange bolts of lights are one of the biggest complaints followed by what appears to be an out-of-control tractor-trailer with a mad trucker, also known by locals as a serial killer, behind the wheel while emblazed in an inferno, barreling straight for you down the highway, and then it just suddenly disappears into thin air.

One survivor of the mad trucker's rampage tells a vivid account of the gory details involving the sadistic semi and how it targets innocent drivers by scaring the hell out of them with its overpowering size and stance while appearing to run them over while engulfed in a fiery hell of speed and position that is sure to annihilate any vehicle into utter ruins or altogether in a state of total nonexistence.

Unsuspecting motorists who have stopped alongside the highway and gotten out of their vehicles to stretch their legs have filed reports on what appears to be packs of demon dogs on the prowl looking for their next kill. Their piercing howls, yellow menacing eyes and razor sharp fanged teeth are a potential danger to anyone that dares to stop in their territory in Utah's extension of the darkened highway to hell.

Reports from all four states have included the sighting of a young woman walking down the highway in only a white nightgown. She literally appears out of nowhere, and whenever anyone attempts to stop and offer her assistance she vanishes right in front of your eyes. The ghost woman has been seen by thousands of motorists, and sometimes she reappears at different locations along the haunted highway to the same driver while traveling across the states from New Mexico to Utah.

Time loss seems to be something of a big deal on this highway since it seems to happen more often then not. Many people believe that time loss is a common symptom when in close proximity to anti-gravity systems that utilize bends in space and time for the propulsion of UFO's. In some cases, people have been known to disappear for a short period of time and again reappearing with no recollection of their time missing or even what had occurred.

This unexplained phenomena has been reported through history from thousands of travelers who have crossed paths with the haunted U.S. state route. Stories from the Native Americans living in the area include the appearance of apparitions showing up in the backseat of tired and unsuspecting motorists, causing them to swerve and in some cases wreck. Strange orbs floating across the highway have also been spotted, especially late at night when traveling alone.

Another legend speaks of the mind boggling and trick playing shape-shifters, skin-walkers or evil shaman also appearing out of nowhere, scaring drivers out of their mind and directly into the path of oncoming traffic causing unexplained accidents along certain parts of the highway.

It is common knowledge that the number 6 to the Navajo Indians, along with any combination of the number 6 is considered evil and to be a harbinger of bad luck. When driving along any section of the haunted highway it is always a good idea to have one or more passengers to travel with you as to eliminate the chances of the more malevolent spirits hitching a ride as ghosts do prefer to have their own seat.

The number of unexplained accidents, paranormal and UFO sightings along with the many fatalities resulting from vehicle related crashes it was becoming impossible to ignore the events on highway 666. With many considerations and only one resolution in hand, in 2003 the Governor delivered a message discussing the end of the remaining sections of route 666.

With the New Mexico State Highway and Transportation Department on board, they two finally joined with Colorado and Utah transportation officials in submitting a final recommendation to eliminate the last remaining sections of the dangerous U.S. 666 and establishing a new route to take its place. The newly named route is now U.S. 491. Old historic signs with the famous route 666 are still in place today as a reminder to what once was, and also serves to aid travelers who have older atlases as their travel guides.

Unfortunately a number change cannot break a curse, and call it what you want, route 666 will forever be in the minds of the people that it has directly affected. Route 666 has and continues to receive so much attention and recognition from the large numbers of strange events that the staggering facts simply can not be ignored.

The haunted and sometimes evil highway has caught plenty of media attention including from the popular USA Today. In 1990 they reported a quote from a State Trooper who claimed that one drunken-driving suspect on U.S. 666 told him, that the "Triple 6 is purely evil. Everyone dies on that highway." In 2002, eleven motorists were killed in car wrecks on U.S. route 666 in New Mexico, and since then the highway was renamed Route 491 due to it being the fourth route off U.S. 191.

The Wall Street Journal jumped on the bandwagon and titled an article "Beast of a Highway, Does Asphalt Stretch Have Biblical Curse?" The article referred to the dangers the highway imposed to motorists and the article quoted a resident saying, "who blames Satan?"

In 1998 the haunted highway was the subject of a cartoon in The New Yorker's issue with a convertible Corvette passing the U.S. 666 sign. Ironically the driver and his passenger are depicted as satanic figures. The movie industry picked up on the innuendos and 2001 Lions Gate Home Entertainment released the movie "Route 666" staring Lou Diamond Phillips. The Supernatural featured Route 666 in 2006, episode 13, season 1 when Dean was contacted by his first love.

Pennsylvania Ghosts: Born on June 16th of 1873, Clara Ida Price was the daughter of David and Margaret Price of Karthaus. During the fall of 1889, Clara had been seen out walking along a footpath, heading towards the Susquehanna River where she was later attacked, raped and then murdered. Clara never had the chance to tell her family and friends goodbye.

State route 879 was not always a well traveled road, in fact it was at one time nothing more than a dirt path that was frequented by locals traveling by horse and buggy or more commonly in those days, by foot. During the fall of 1889, during the Thanksgiving holiday, Clara had been seen out walking along the path, heading towards the Susquehanna River.

Many unsuspecting folks traveling down state route 879, near Karthaus Pennsylvania, have become acquainted with the ghost of Clara Price, who is known to walk these parts early in the morning. By most accounts, she is friendly and unassuming, and her lovely presence is hard to ignore. The beautiful sixteen year old with the flowing head of hair was at the prime of her life when she was viciously murdered by thieving scoundrel, Alfred Andrews, an Englishman from Ponsanooth, Cornwall, England.

Several people had spotted the young beauty that day, including the highly respected Mrs. Watson who by all accounts was a constant source of current local happenings and didn't easily miss something as unnatural as a dirty, smooth faced, stocky man donning a derby hat, following the young Clara as she unknowingly walked among the peaceful setting that surrounded her. Her lifeless body was discovered sprawled out on the desolate road that was embedded with muddy terrain in a way that was unbecoming to those who knew and loved the friendly teenager.

Alfred relocated to the area after learning that he could become gainfully employed due to the immense bed of coke and iron ore where the manufacturing of pig iron was made. Alfred was known for being a bit unsavory, unpolished and by most accounts, inferior to other men. Because of these traits, he held many jobs and never remained in one place for long. He had a reputation for being a thief with a sad lack of moral boundaries, and even though he was married, he had an eye for the ladies, especially young, pretty ones.

It was quickly discovered that the young beauty had been shot in the head several times. Later, upon examining Clara's body, it was quickly uncovered that she had been raped. Witnesses stepped forward, claiming that a short, stocky man in a brown derby hat had been seen in the area where her body was discovered.

Several other witnesses soon came forward, giving the same description of a man that was seen in the vicinity of where Clara had been walking earlier in the day. In no time the police closed in on Alfred Andrews, who clearly matched the description given by the locals.

On the day that Clara was murdered, Alfred had set out on a deliberate stealing spree as a means of providing for his family. He had previously shot a killed a neighbor's pig, to which he later admitted to, but claimed that he would never harm a human. Alfred had high hopes of robbing the general store in Karthaus that day, hiding in the thick woods that bordered the riding trail in an effort to remain hidden from prying eyes as he made his way towards his targeted goal.

Several people had walked the trail that day, and a few of them had noticed Mr. Andrews after he came out of hiding in thwarted attempts at robbing a few of the loaded down peddlers, but opportunity never gave way to the brazen thief. He then spotted the lovely Clara Price walking in his direction. Seeing Alfred, the young woman attempted to step around him by edging towards the woods. Alfred seeing an opportunity to talk to the girl, asked her her name. She responded and began to walk faster, away from Mr. Andrews.

Born on June 16th of 1873, Clara Ida Price was the daughter of David and Margaret Price of Karthaus. At the time of her vicious attack, rape and murder, she had been staying with Mrs. Meeker, a close family friend. After staying at the Meeker home for an undetermined amount of time, Clara had set out for her home in Karthaus early in the morning with a basket of goods in her hand when she was accosted by the evil Andrews.

Having a friendly disposition, it is entirely possible that Alfred Andrews was able to approach Clara quite easily, making it easy for him to manhandle the young girl and later kill her when no one was around. What Mr. Andrews didn't bank on was the numerous eye witnesses that spotted him following the naive young girl in her attempt to return home in an otherwise safe area.

On a cold, damp and foggy day in January, just after six days of deliberation , Alfred Andrews was executed by hanging. Sheriff Robert Cooke, members of the clergy and several deputies escorted the accused up the steps and into a noose that hung several feet above a trap door. A black bag was placed over Alfred's head. The lever was then pulled, dropping the murderer like a sack of potatoes, breaking his neck instantly. His body was placed in an undisclosed location after the cemetery officials refused his body for interment.

The Clara Price Memorial Marks the Site of the 1889 Murder: Today a new memorial marking the site of the murder can be viewed just a half-mile east of the bridge over the West Branch of the Susquehanna River. However it is not her final resting place. Clara Ida Price was laid to rest, nearby at the Keewaydin Cemetery in Covington Township, Clearfield County. Clara's parents, David and Margaret Price were laid to rest beside her three decades later. Clara never had the chance to tell her family and friends goodbye.

In the early morning, cars passing by the area have reported seeing a young, female ghost walking along the area of 879, close to her marker, where she was found murdered over one-hundred years ago. It is believed that she is still attempting to make it home today, but Alfred Andrews prophetic words spoken just before he died concluded his inhumane deed when he loudly stated, "I am sorry I took the life of that girl, and I hope to meet her in heaven." A promise such as this has given the young girl no choice but to keep running away from the man that ended her young life.

Our Visit to a Pittsburgh Bar In 2013: Sitting at a fork in the road in Allegheny County, positioned between USS Clairton Works and the Mon Valley Works Irvin Plant steel mills, on the outskirts of Clairton, Pennsylvania is the historical and haunted Valley Hotel Bar & Grill.

Built in 1863, the Valley Hotel Bar & Grill is not only regularly packed with dedicated patrons, it is filled with a deep history that includes a name change, renovations, fire, flood, and several ghosts. This is the haunted meeting place where barge employees, steel workers, locals, and music enthusiasts flock together for libation, and much needed equilibrium after putting in long hours of physical labor. Everyone who enters the haunted bar enjoys live music, a sense of community and paranormal experiences that are undeniable to those lucky enough to witness the unexplained activity at the Jefferson Borough bar.

The Valley Hotel Bar & Grill was at one time merely a building filled with quiet sleeping quarters for weary workers back when it was originally named the Hotel Granger. The Granger family was the original owners of the Hotel Granger that catered to local riverboat crews, railroad workers and miners.

The hotel displayed their name up until the Traphalis family took over ownership of the historical building that sits near the Monongahela River. The building is no stranger to change, especially after the third floor of the hotel was completely destroyed in 1971 when a fire ripped through the wooden structure. The gutted interior was never replaced, forever changing the features of the historical establishment which was later converted into a two-story building.

Today the Valley Hotel Bar & Grill is owned by Jo Ellen Oggier and Bill "Duel" Deemer, who purchased the haunted establishment in 2004. The couple is constantly receiving reports on unexplained paranormal activity and strange incidents from various sources concerning orbs, ghosts, moving objects, and eerily haunting voices from friendly ghosts attempting to join the party.

The paranormal activity seemed to heighten in the 1970s during the time of renovations to which paranormal investigators claim go with the territory of periods of transition. Investigators from the Pittsburgh Paranormal Society were asked to take a deeper look at the reality of ghosts on the premises and found that activity coming from the spirits was a definite possibility after they captured the evidence on film.

After spending a whole night at the Valley Hotel, the paranormal team discovered a spirit sitting next to one of the investigators after studying pictures taken at the bar and random orbs were found all over the photos in various locations throughout the building. The group also discovered that ethereal faces suddenly appear in the large mirror and disappear before you can wrap your mind around what is happening right in front of you.

While in the basement, which is described by most visitors, including local maintenance man, Bert Wright, as unequivocally eerie where strange activities take place, including sightings of dark shadows and disembodied voices. Other incidences involving the basement occurred during a paranormal investigation when the team heard what sounded like a mirror shattering.

The spirits and their phenomena are evident in just about everything from the phantom footsteps that can openly be heard even though nobody is physically there to floating balls of light that glow. The biggest mystery surrounds objects disappearing and then reappearing weeks later and the unexplained ghost voices coming from the basement that sound as though a couple are arguing.

The owners claim that there are no evil spirits, poltergeists or malevolent ghosts lurking about, but try telling that to local resident Elliot Jones, who was scared so badly by the ghosts that he refuses to come back. Elliot had a standing monthly appointment at the hotel to which he would collect aluminum cans from the basement's recycling chute.

Never in his wildest dreams did he expect to hear the blood curdling scream coming from a female ghost calling out for help. Elliot lost all composure and fled the area. He never looked back, but felt he needed to report the incident to the owners as many other visitors to the bar has done over the last decade.

Infrared cameras have picked up floating formations that appear in an arc position spreading out from the bar to the kitchen and almost appear as if there are ghosts partaking in a friendly game of volleyball when studied closely. The second floor is famous for footsteps coming from the third floor which is no longer there, and unexplained voices from unseen entities are a constant companion despite the area being void of humans and it is now used for storage.

The history of the Valley Hotel Bar & Grill is somewhat a mystery as very little has been documented in the way of death, disaster or other reasons that the ghosts have taken up residency at the historical establishment, but the owners and patrons really don't mind and feel that it adds to the character of the building.

Live Bands: The Valley Hotel Bar & Grill is the very essence of Steel City pride where the musicians come to play on a brand new stage complete with Duel's awesome guitar collection and an array of equipment. Popular local bands play every Saturday night and musicians are welcome to stop in for open stage jam sessions on Friday nights.

Location: 1004 New England Hollow Road, Clairton, Pennsylvania.

You've Got Ghosts: Let's face it, a ghost or spirit doesn't take up much room, but if you really want them gone, smudge your new home with sage. If this ancient and sacred ceremony fails, call in the professionals.

Paranormal investigators will put forth every effort to solve the homes manifestation issues since experienced and reliable ghost hunters can either debunk or prove the presence of ghosts and spirits in your humble abode. The site, Etsy sells a variety of smudge kits for your paranormal and personal cleansing needs.

Skeptics will tell you that there is just no such thing as ghostly phenomena, but in reality the likelihood that ghosts do exist has been proven time and time again, making even the skeptics question what really is going on in their home. Even shows like HGTV cannot ignore the obvious.... that being new home owners questioning strange events taking place within their new space, and the only reasonable answer is that the joint is haunted.

Of course the majority of people resort to the notion that ghosts living in the home are nothing more then friendly entities that stare back at you in the mirror, bang around the attic, causing harmless chaos and getting into things that they shouldn't, quite often causing objects to be temporarily misplaced.

One couple who openly admit to being skeptical when it comes to ghosts aren't so sure how they feel about paranormal activity after they dealt with it first hand in their new digs in Germantown, Ohio. Their Story: Matt and Jennifer Chambers learned that ghosts can in fact communicate with the living, and they clearly can take on a voice similar to those around them that are living. Not long after the couple purchased their new home, they had a brush with what can only be described as someone from the other side attempting to call their cat Mukky.

As Jennifer was telling the feline to kill a ferocious spider her husband Matt clearly heard a man's voice also talking to the cat. The only problem is that there was no other man in the house. Jennifer also heard the male voice, but assumed that it was her husband mumbling under his breath. After questioning neighbors the couple learned that the voice probably belonged to the prior homeowner who had recently passed from cancer while under the care of hospice.

The possibilities are endless. What now...sell front row tickets to your new haunted house, live in fear, call the police, hold a séance or when all else has failed, put the ghost-infested ramshackle of a home up for sale?

According to the experts, the answer lies squarely with each individual owner and how they feel about living with spirits. The majority of people are going to fear the unknown, so getting a better understanding of who lived in your home before you and how they passed on is a great place to start.

After all you have just shelled out a lot of money on your new place. It would be a real shame to be too afraid to enjoy it because of a few pesky ghosts. The key is to try and calm down and listen to what the spirits may be trying to tell you. It could be everything from a warning about the house to the ghost attempting to tell you how the met their demise.

Malevolent ghosts, demons and dark entities are of an entirely different nature. These ill disposed entities are not to be taken lightly and often require the need to call in a Priest, especially when the events are so overwhelming that it is causing a loss of sleep to actual damages to humans or the home itself.

In most cases living with ghosts can actually be entertaining. Most active ghosts will do everything within their power to make their presence known by doing everything from showing up in unexpected places in an actual form that simulates a human to making a loud racket to get your attention.

Many ghosts are playful and will move objects or open cupboards. When ghosts become overly annoying you may have to remind them that you now live in the home and would appreciate it if they would respect your house with a bit of quiet time. Ask them want they want or need, and remind them that you are fully aware that they are there, but that there are rules of the house that they must also follow if they wish to remain living in your home. Try to keep in mind that they were once living beings that are lost and simply need guidance in finding their way home.

Strange odors sometimes present themselves when a ghost or spirit has entered the room. Popular smells associated with good ghosts include flowers, tobacco, food, and perfume. Foul smells like rotten eggs, burning matches, sulfur, rotten meat, and fire are not to be taken lightly. In fact this is a bigger problem then most people can handle without some form of outside help.

Burning sage and sprinkling your home with salt is the best way to eliminate evil spirits, but for those stubborn poltergeists and demons that refuse to leave, an exorcism is about the only thing left to do. If you become afraid of the circumstances going on then quickly make your own presence known and clearly state to the spirited intruder that they are in fact scaring you, and tell the ghost to please stop it.

Some ghosts enjoy the soothing sound of a television or stereo, and this was precisely the case determined when Toni Cusumano was enjoying a quiet evening at home alone watching her favorite program in her sprawling haunted Victorian mansion located in the Pennsylvania

Poconos. All of a sudden Toni heard the television in her son's room spring to life.

Toni was snug as a bug in her most comfortable chair, and by no means wanting to get up and investigate the issue at hand, so she loudly yelled, "knock it off" to which she was quickly rewarded with sudden and complete silence from the upstairs bedroom. She claims that the problem has since been solved.

Many ghosts are mischievous in nature and only want you to acknowledge them by talking to them and often times they will openly show up and appear to you as a regular human in form. They can also appear as a full-bodied, non-vaporous see-through appearance of a disembodied person's spirit, also known as an apparition. In this instance most people react to their presence similarly to those actors seen in the movie Casper or Ghost Busters. Try to calm down and ask them to leave because they are scaring you. Most good ghosts are polite and will abide by your wishes.

Florida based ghost hunters, Scott Flagg and Jack Roth have investigated hundreds of cases of haunted homes around the world. Through their experiences they have learned that when it comes to ghosts in the home, living with a benevolent ghost is perfectly fine so long as they do not bring harm to the people living at the residence in question. Many people transition quite well in a home filled with kindred spirits and come to the conclusion that the ghosts protect and watch over their loved ones.

Conversations With the Dead: Imagine a spirit world existing in Small-town, America where you are immediately uplifted the moment you cross the town line. Everyday life is positive and the gifted people of the community work and live in harmony. It is not fantasy, it is a way of life, and you are invited to experience this unique and healing path of virtue by exploring Lily Dale, New York yourself. The Lily Dale assembly proudly displays a sign representing it to be "the world's largest center for the religion of spiritualism," despite the town having a abnormally small population of just 275 citizens year round.

The community is located within the town of Pomfret, found in the southwestern corner of New York next to Cassadaga Lake that is well known for psychic mediums, clairvoyants, prayer, church services, religious and healing services and it is a major backdrop for the paranormal. Thousands of people flock to Lily Dale to embrace spiritual awareness, uplifting lectures and to speak with one of the many mediums that live in the town. Psychic medium John Edward and Spiritual medium James Van Praagh are frequent visitors of Lily Dale, and offer private appointments and give regular lectures.

The quaint serenity of the community that embraces the power of free will and openly communicating with the dead is embellished with Victorian gingerbread style homes reminiscent of a different era, but among the many treasures you will find is an atmosphere filled with energy, yet has clearly not been marred by charlatans or self-proclaimed psychic fortune-tellers, tea-leaf, palm or crystal ball readers promising divine destinies and impossible dreams for a large sum of money.

Known as the town that talks to the dead, "Lilly Dale" was founded in 1879 by sisters Margaret and Kate Fox, role models and leaders of the creation of Spiritualism. The town was later named Lily Dale, possibly due to the massive amounts of lilies found growing around the nearby area of the lake. The original cottage of founders Margaret and Kate Fox was moved to Lily Dale in 1916 from nearby Hydesville, giving the community instant recognition for Spiritualism overnight. By 1927 Lily Dale had an official postal name and zip code.

Lily Dale Ghost Walks: Every year on Wednesdays, from July 3 through August 28, Lily Dale residents and visitors will meet at the auditorium for a scheduled ghost walk that leads you on a tour mixed with history and the stuff legends are made of. The medium guide will touch on etheric energy, which he claims all humans possess. It can be greatly improved by healthy eating and an energized aura that is vitalized by deep breathing.

The energy evaporates, but can remain when strong emotion is connected to them. Some people can pick up on it and actually see this energy that has been left behind. While learning about etheric energy, you will pass several of the well known haunted grounds where spirit's reside and stroll.

You will experience the spirit lights that are often detected when passing the Healing Temple, and a visit to the historic museum brings forth unanswered questions as to the identity of the unseen hands that magically transported paint to a canvas, applying itself via a mist during a gathering.

The granddaddy of all has to be "Inspiration Stump," the virtual energy vortex located in the historic Leolyn Woods that has been the heart of communication with the dead and delivering spiritual messages since 1898.

Location: Lily Dale Auditorium, Cottage Row, Melrose Park, Lily Dale, New York

Angel House & Mortal Abode: The awe-inspiring Angel House was built in 1897 and is the quintessential abode when it comes to delightful, beautiful and charming places to stay. The large wrap around porch is dotted with whimsical touches from wizards and angels that invite you in to explore the many displayed treasures found deeper within the premises. Unique themes are featured among the eight different rooms at the abode from an inspirational fairy room to a cleverly thought out heavens and sky room embellished with divine celestial overtures.

Location: At the corner of South and Cleveland Streets in Lily Dale, New York, 14752. Closed: From September until May the Angel House is closed.

Edgar Allan Poe's Grave 2019: We have visited this site on a few locations. So far it has been quiet, but it has been documented as being one of the most haunted destinations in the United States....The Westminster Burial Grounds is considered to be one of the most haunted cemeteries in the United States. It is occupied with famous and restless walking corpses from generals and mayors to influential businessmen and writers. One of those famous writers, often referred to as the dark poet aka Edgar Allan Poe, refuses to believe that he is dead and makes every attempt to demonstrate this by showing up on his birthday every year since his death in 1849.

Once you step foot into the ethereal and antiquated cemetery, there is absolutely no question that you have just wandered into a place where nothing living could possibly exist in a natural state. You also realize that the forbidden eeriness of the dark shadows lurking about instantly chill your bones and the raunchy stench remotely resembles that of a rotting corpse.

It has been considered one of the most haunted cemeteries in the United States due to the high amount of paranormal activity witnessed by people simply walking past it. Depending on whom you are and your thought process over haunted destinations and active dark spirits, the Western Burial Ground of the Westminster Presbyterian Church yard in Baltimore, Maryland could be considered one of the best cemeteries to visit or it could be on your list of worst nightmare vacation destinations.

Dark legends filled with shocking truths have permanently scarred the Westminster Presbyterian Western Burial Ground in Baltimore, Maryland since it was originally constructed in 1786. The church was built directly over the burial grounds, and finally completed in 1852, but the structures original massive arches created underground catacombs that have been a constant source of supernatural occurrences and other unexplained phenomena, both below and above ground.

Over time bodies were constantly disarranged and even removed from their original resting place in an effort to accommodate the strict policies that city officials once enforced in the mid 1800's. Medical students also took part in these disturbances as dissecting bodies was a common practice in gaining medical knowledge. Soldiers from the civil war took refuge within the catacombs and stored weapons and other gear within the tombs.

Safety and health concerns that loomed within Baltimore's city limits soon became apparent, and cemeteries were to be accompanied by a church. This posed a slight problem as the burial grounds already existed. Underground pathways ran amuck underneath the busy city streets, but these passageways were often times the only access to buried loved ones.

If visiting with the young ghost of forty year-old Edgar Allan Poe intrigues you, then this is the place to be in the middle of winter. He has been spotted on various accounts, but most sightings are around his birth date of January 19th. The Raven is completely dressed in a black wool waistcoat and trousers, donning a wide brimmed black hat, and a dark scarf wrapped around his face, possibly to hide it from the view of curious gawkers. His solid cat's head walking stick can be heard tapping against the hard ground of the earth as he strolls through the cemetery.

Ghostly tales that have sustained surround the fact that many of these restless souls wandering the burial grounds were buried in the cemetery alive. Once they passed over to the spiritual side, their spirit began to wander the grounds while seeking out the person or group of people that buried them alive in order to get revenge for putting them through such a savage death. There are quite a few unsettled spirits at this haunted graveyard who seem to be forever looking for something that they just cannot find, and they often frighten the individuals that stumble upon them during their search.

Many paranormal experts believe that the problem exists within the original construction and lay-out of the burial grounds and the church. Not all of the deceased can be properly visited due to bad planning. Some of the headstones are unreadable due to their age, and visitors to the cemetery are unaware of the hard to find parts of the graveyard that have been partially covered by the massive Gothic Revival- style Westminster Church. The hidden underground catacombs are the only access to some of the most restless souls on the planet.

Muffled screams from a seemingly bottomless dark pit from an unknown destination found deep below the earth can be heard and compared to as a personal human hell simply from the depth of the anguish felt by the living when hearing their tortured screams. Ghosts and restless spirits aimlessly roam the dark underground passageways of the catacombs that are encompassed by a foul stench, and a white haired entity is often seen walking slowly through the grave markers in apparent search of something.

Rumors, legends and ghost stories have remained a part of the cemeteries rich history due to actual communication and ghost sightings by living beings visiting the burial grounds. Amateur ghost hunters, paranormal investigators, physics and thrill seekers quite often experience paranormal activity by talking and communicating almost telepathically with those who have crossed over and are now part of the spirit world just by visiting the massive grounds that holds them prisoner. These lonely spirits appear to be anxious to tell their story and visit with the living souls that may finally accomplish putting them to rest at last.

The Western Burial Ground of the Westminster Presbyterian Church yard in Baltimore, Maryland has had its share of paranormal investigators, but there is no doubt that Edgar Allan Poe's birthday is by far one of the hottest peaks for communicating with the dead. Curator Jeff Jerome invited 70 guests and one photographer to gather at the grave site of the famous poet on his birthday. They celebrated by reading his works, and drank dark amontillado sherry to emulate a featured drink from one of Poe's many horror stories.

The photographer waited patiently for the moment that a ghostly encounter would occur, and before he could say cheese, the entire group witnessed the spirit of a light haired man dressed in black running through the cemetery carrying a cane. He kneeled down at the poet's grave; then quietly vanished into the dark night air. They later reported that the ghost wore a period frock coat, and they found that flowers had been placed on his grave. Life magazine featured the haunting picture that was captured by infrared night-vision equipment, and the experts deemed the photo of the entity as a real spirit.

Several other encounters with ghosts have been reported by ghost hunters and paranormal investigators looking for proof that the dead walk among us, but many visitors of the burial grounds are there to pay their respects. It would appear however that the spirit world has repugnance for living souls as they are often taunted by the spirits living there. The casualties of war included Generals Samuel Smith and John Stricker, who were both laid to rest at the Westminster Presbyterian Western Burial Ground.

Lucia Watson Taylor: Sixteen year old Lucia Watson Taylor is a frequent visitor of the cemetery, especially if it is dark and misty. Her white flowing dress is hard to miss, as is her beautiful head of long hair. The problem with this vision is that she crossed over in late 1816, but she has been seen praying within the burial grounds on many an occasion. Dark figures, hazy spirits, ghostly sightings, footsteps, screams, laughing, and indescribable rancid odors are all a part of these older then dirt resting grounds that never rests.

Over time bodies have been disturbed from their original resting place in an effort to accommodate the strict policies that city officials once enforced in the mid 1800's. Safety and health concerns that loomed within Baltimore's city limits soon became apparent, and cemeteries were to be accompanied by a church. This posed a slight problem as the burial grounds already existed.

The grandfather of President James Buchanan attempts to rest in the confines of this highly spirited playground for ghosts, and several unsavory spirits roam the grounds in an effort to chase off disrespectful thrill seekers that refuse to keep the noise at a level that allows the spirits to sleep. Generals, soldiers, statesmen, politicians and crazed lunatic, Leona Wellesley are all buried deep within the deep rich soils of the 18th-century style burial grounds; however they have undoubtedly left the confines of their wooden boxes that housed them upon final viewing, and are now walking among the many visitors that have come to see them.

A letter by Edgar Allan Poe to Frederick W. Thomas, written on February 14, 1849, states: Depend upon it, after all, Thomas, Literature is the most noble of professions. In fact, it is about the only one fit for a man. For my own part, there is no seducing me from the path."

Location: 519 West Fayette Street, Baltimore, Maryland.

2008, Beaver, Pennsylvania: Hidden deep within the heart of Beaver County, Pennsylvania remain a few questionable mysteries, along with a couple of ghosts in what was once known as Mudlick Hollow, located just outside of the once thriving town of Vanport, Pennsylvania. The town and hollow still remain, but its days of bustling are long gone. The river bank was once home to many Indian tribes who camped while nourishing themselves from the hearty fish filled waters while watching for any enemies from the lookout point at Bear Hill.

Artifacts and relics are all that remains of the Indian burial grounds, located in Beaver County, that and strange noises that can be heard on foggy nights from passerby's out on a leisurely walk. The eeriness is hard to pinpoint though as many tragedies have stricken Vanport throughout time, even from the very beginning of its construction.

Due to the many creeks filled by the larger Ohio River that flow through the area, Vanport became a prime location for small boats, and eventually a ferry. Thomas B. Boggs began planning the town of Vanport in 1835 on the north bank of the Ohio River, to which unbeknownst to him was laden with lime rather then the coke he was hoping for.

The many rough hills were the only thing that stood in the way of a bridge, railroad, and eventually homesteads that would complete Vanport, making it a thriving community. Unfortunately a multitude of accidents and deaths happened during the construction of the town, as heavy equipment was not readily available, leaving overworked men to depend on less sophisticated tools.

A church, post office, mercantile, and a few other businesses were quickly built as the town thrived from the four potteries kept busy with the newly discovered lime. The need for a ferry was obvious and work on the piers began where the Two Mile Creek empties into the Ohio River. Two major lime kilns were located west of the ferry. Other potteries were owned by prominent resident John Weaver of Mudlick Hollow, located a stone's throw from Vanport down an isolated dirt road.

Another prominent resident known by the town's people as kind and gentle was J.J. Noss. He quickly made plans for a grand estate to be erected and located just up the road from Patrick Mulvanen's grand mansion in Mudlick Hollow, located less than a mile from the busier town of Vanport. He felt that this was a prime location for a second mansion as the area was leveled off and surrounded by a bounty of large trees. Both estates were built for the men's fiancés, and by 1846 the mansion's stood completed.

Patrick designed a stately mansion for his fiancé Anna Mines. The plans included large white pillars, which gave it the name of the "White House" by residents of Vanport. Each room was immense and embellished with beautifully carved fire-places, and a huge ornate stairway led to the third floor which offered two large bedrooms. The entire east end of the house was one large ball room, designed with Anna in mind as she loved to throw extravagant parties.

The marriage was to never be as Anna fell to her death while walking down the ornate stairway, breaking her neck and leaving Patrick in a state that was less then desirable to onlookers. Cries can be heard from the wooded area of Mudlick Hollow on foggy nights, and many have wondered if it was Patrick himself crying out in disbelief as he stared death in the eye on the fateful night that he witnessed his true love taking her last breath. Other tragedies would follow, but perhaps none was more devastating then that of the newly wed couple that met with death on a dark and foggy night in Mudlick Hollow.

After taking a wrong turn on one of the many dirt roads that runs throughout Mudlick Hollow, a bride and groom riding in their horse drawn buggy on their way home from their wedding steered off of course and attempted to regain the correct trail to their new home. The horses quickly became spooked by noises coming from the woods causing the buggy to roll off the road and into the creek.

The bride died immediately from a broken neck while the groom became pinned under the carriage, later dying from his injuries sustained in the crash. The residents of Vanport claim that on dark nights of the new moon as fog creeps up onto the dirt lane you can hear a horse drawn buggy approaching from absolutely nowhere, and before it comes into contact with the one who hears it, you will hear a crash, followed by a scream, then the dark night becomes eerily silent once again.

Location: The haunted woods of Mudlick Hollow are located just two minutes from Vanport, Pennsylvania, just off of highway 68 west. Make a sharp right just after the bridge onto Division Lane, and then an immediate left onto Mudlick Hollow Road. The mansions have become the property of the Beaver Valley Expressway as plans for highway 60 took precedence over historical monuments.

Elizabeth, Pennsylvania 2017: Sheltered among the trees along the Monongahela River, just 15 miles south of Pittsburgh, early travelers located some of the most fertile soil and picturesque landscape that they had ever laid their eyes on. A simply amazing discovery, the area was not only perfect for boat and ship building, but it offered a hub for various forms for incorporating businesses in the area, and it offered conditions perfect for sustaining during the heat of summer and the brutal winters that western Pennsylvania is known for.

Sometime during the mid to late 1700s, settlers from New Jersey, Maryland and Delaware began moving into the area now known as Elizabeth, Pennsylvania, taking advantage of the lush foliage and generous farmland that sat nestled between Brownsville and Pittsburgh, two cities bustling with riverfront transportation and glass making businesses during a time when migration and community development was in it's infancy. Elizabeth, Pennsylvania was named after Elizabeth Mackay Bayard, the wife of Colonel Stephen Bayard, who along with Elizabeth's brother, Samuel Mackay, founded the town in 1787.

Elizabeth later became the bustling borough that it is still known for today in 1834. Elizabeth is most famous for boat building and is known for having been visited by the famous pioneers, Lewis and Clark, and the highly accomplished Capt. John Walker was more than likely contracted to build the fifty-five foot keel boat aka "big boat" that was used in the Lewis and Clark expedition.

While many will argue that the "big boat" was built in the boatyard near the Liberty Bridge in Pittsburgh, the mystery of where the big boat was built according to the founding fathers of Elizabeth, was built at the edge of the Monongahela River and later the durable merchant vessel set sail from the shipyard based in Elizabeth.

One later account of the origins of the famous keel boat carrying Lewis & Clark came directly from a reliable source during an interview with Col. George A. Bayard, son of Col. Stephen Bayard in early 1852. Col. Bayard was reported as stating that the early involvement of boat building included the famous keel boat that was built by John Walker at the boatyard located along the waterfront in Elizabeth Borough, confirming the previous historical documentation involving the paper trail of the Lewis and Clark expedition.

Today, Elizabeth has many more mysteries that embody the town with intrigue and is a definite place of interest for anyone who loves history, paranormal activity, beauty, fine dining, dancing in the streets, and that welcoming small town feel that a community like Elizabeth offers.

Elizabeth, once known as Elizabeth Town, is the second oldest town in Allegheny County and is known for being home to the first ship building industry west of the Allegheny Mountains. It wasn't long before the town became famous for her very own ship, the "Monongahela Farmer" who sailed from Elizabeth to New Orleans in 1800.

Towboats nudging barges filled with coal along the river, work and pleasure boats, water sports, music, history, festivals, and a variety of excellent cuisine are all a huge part of what makes Elizabeth the bustling community that it is today. It is quite possible that the festivities are so lively that even the ghosts travel down from "Town Hill" to be included in the activities in the heart of the town where music, dancing in the streets, festivities, fine dining, and highly spirited celebrations occur down on Plum Street, Second Avenue and Water Street.

Plum Street, Elizabeth is a favorite pass time for locals and tourists who enjoy a variety of music. Plum Street closes down to traffic and opens up to those who desire to dance in the street for some summer fun. A variety of bands blast the town with tunes that lure in the crowds every Thursday night to the "Sounds of Summer."

Rockwell's Red Lion Restaurant at the corner of Plum Street and Second Avenue has been a favorite upscale dining choice since 1980. Spirited banquets featuring weddings and Christmas parties and other festive occasions are celebrated events that can be found regularly in the lower level of the famous restaurant, located in the "Lion's Den."

The Grand Theatre, located on Second Avenue, next to the Rockwell's Red Lion Restaurant is the perfect location for paranormal activity. Ghosts enjoy being around people and this building is constantly filled with activity. Dark shadows, unexplained noises and voices have all been a part of the theatrical experience even after the last performer has exited the building and the doors have been locked.

Walking past the theater, strange forms have appeared in the windows and apparitions have been seen inside of the building from various sources. Perhaps it is the ghost of Elizabeth Bayard, merely seeking a night of entertainment, away from the humdrum of the dark and quiet surroundings found just up the hill at the haunted cemetery where her soul is forever lost. The July Riverfest in Elizabeth is another crowd pleaser that draws in thousands of spectators who enjoy good food, live music, festivities, fireworks, boats, competitions, first-responder demonstrations, and a parade.

Unfortunately all towns have their scars and secrets, and Elizabeth is no exception to this rule. The Borough of Elizabeth is known for having a historical cemetery that is considered a "Disgrace to Elizabeth." This historic cemetery is where the founding fathers of the town are buried. Historians will find the graves of Walker, McClure, Penniman, Lynch, Mitchell, and the VanKirk family.

These are just a few of the first pioneers who settled in the area and would eventually be buried in the very place they called home. Their grave sites can be found among the trees in the upper section of the cemetery, untouched by time, severe winters and overgrown weeds. This famous cemetery was also once the final resting place for Elizabeth Mackay Bayard, for whom the town was named.

Sadly, bad planning that included the decision to uproot and remove old graves from the "Old Cemetery" and place them into the Elizabeth Cemetery was a disaster resulting in several mounds of broken tombstones and lost graves. The planned removal caused considerable chaos and the loss of many headstones and bodies. This monumental disaster is noted in the October 4, 1889 issue, claiming that the number of bodies removed from the Old Graveyard is much larger than most people had suspected and is a disgrace to the town of Elizabeth. The Elizabeth Cemetery, located on Cemetery Road is the final resting place for more than eighty-two Civil War veterans.

Ghosts have a way of getting their point across in the only way that they know how. Severe distress at the "Old Graveyard" was causing concern to all that visited. An abundance of appearances from unsettled ghosts and misguided apparitions, summoning for some type of reckoning to anyone who would listen that help was desperately needed for those lost souls that were so easily forgotten about.

Reports of orbs, glowing lights, dark shadows and eerie sounds were becoming a steady occurrence at the Old Graveyard nestled between Tanner Aly, Bayard Street and 5th Avenue. Fear of the unknown kept citizens away from the cemetery grounds, hidden high on top of the hill, under the protection of the shade trees, up until the late seventies, when the heavily overgrown cemetery was almost impossible to walk through.

Through the years complaints to the city flooded in from family members of those who were buried in the destroyed remnants of what used to be the final resting place of their loved ones, but is now nothing more than a few graves surrounded by a bungled mess. The lack of detail and loss of loved ones, poor record keeping and the total disregard to the family's when it came time to exhume and transfer the remains to an entirely different grave site forced the community to jump into action over a distressing issue that was simply not going to go away.

Historians, Della and Frank Fischer were called in to decipher what headstones they could read and volunteers cleaned, mowed and reset the remaining headstones. Many of the grave sites have no stones, including the grave marker for Elizabeth Bayard, that is presently, forever lost.

Elizabeth borough today has a population of nearly 1,500 citizens. At the corner of Bayard Street and 5th Avenue, there is a lined trail that will lead you to the handful of the last few graves that have been left behind, most of which contain Elizabeth's founding fathers. The rest of the broken mounds of rubble left behind from discarded tombstones is all that remain of the "Old Graveyard."

The "Old Cemetery" remains as a reminder to those who built the town and put it on the map. The entrance to grave sites still remains. Steps with a historic marker greet you as you walk up the hill towards the remaining headstones. Some are intact while several others are dumped in an unorganized mound of crumbles that leaves us wondering where the restless spirits of those spirits that were tossed about so haphazardly could be found roaming today.

Are they forever stuck in transition or were these restless spirits eventually capable of overcoming such blatant disregard and ignorance and put their muddled burial mishap behind them. Many residents still claim that there are ghosts residing on top of the hill of the "Old Graveyard" while others simply do not believe that paranormal activity is the cause of the many unexplained events that take place when the moon is void and the night is as black as the coal that surrounds the town that houses it.

The Borough of Elizabeth is a thriving community filled with businesses that are a mirror of days gone by. History repeats itself in everyday life and in many of the historic buildings where ghosts and spirits make themselves heard in sound and presence, attempting to contribute themselves, still wishing to be an active part of the town where they once lived and worked. Paranormal activity is evident in many of the older buildings where workers labored and etched their names into the many pieces of what makes Elizabeth still flourish today.

Second Street offers historians and ghost hunters a glimpse into the heart and history of Elizabeth. Many of the business owners along this main thoroughfare claim that paranormal activity has long been a part of the town's charisma. The old warehouse located under the Malady bridge that now houses the Elizabeth Beer Distributor was once a church. Echoes of the past are heard at different hours throughout the day and night at the historic building. Disembodied footsteps, dark shadows and strange voices keep the staff on their toes, but just like the residents of Elizabeth, the ghosts are friendly and welcome customers to come in for a spirited visit.

Just before midnight, during the new moon on August 14, our small group of ghost hunters conducted a paranormal investigation. Ascending the steps of the "Old Graveyard, we noted that the air felt cooler despite it being a relatively warm evening. Previously, on our walk towards the haunted cemetery, the night showed promise of an eerie sort quiet and calm, but once we got to the middle of the hill on Bayard Street at the entrance to the muddled mess of broken graves we found that the grounds were anything but silent.

After reaching the furthest point in the cemetery along the fence and the alley, along the back side of the cemetery, we all noticed the strong odor reminiscent of roses. The smell was so prominent that it immediately overpowered the entire area. The bizarre anomaly was accompanied by footsteps coming from the tree area where the Penniman tombstone sits.

At the same moment, the EMF spiked, and the temperatures dropped for several seconds, detecting a strange energy force. The cameras picked up several orbs and with them came the odd sensation of not being able to breathe due to the air becoming thick and permeated by a strange mist.

Within a few minutes the graveyard returned to normal even though none of us could quite shake the overwhelming feeling of being watched by someone or something that was undetectable to the human eye. With these discoveries came an unsettling feeling, yet there was never a threat of danger, only an overpowering sensation of a peaceful calm, possibly due to acknowledgment and the existence of truth that was once forever buried on a lonely hill.

Murrysville, Pennsylvania 2016: Erected in 1817, the old historic church that once sat on Hankey Church Road has become clouded through the years with various tales and a haunting legend surrounding a minister who once reportedly tormented several of the members of the Hankey Church sometime during the mid-1800s. The church along with a log cabin was located in the grassy clearing directly across the road from the picturesque white-picket-fence ensconced entrance to the historic Hankey Cemetery before it burned completely to the ground in 1973.

The area where the church once sat so many years ago today has a diabolical feeling that is highly charged with an active energy that is nearly impossible to dismiss. These problematic entities could be the result of visitors, thrill seekers and ghost hunters trespassing into the church with attempts to summon evil spirits with frivolous child's play during long sessions with the Ouija board.

According to local folklore, if you have experienced the feeling of being touched while on the old church grounds, you have more than likely come into contact with the spirit of the minister who haunts the Hankey Church Road cemetery and nearby property, located in the heart of the Appalachian Mountains in the city of Murrysville, Pennsylvania, approximately 20 miles from Pittsburgh.

Despite the origins of the angry energy, once you have decided to tread upon the old church grounds, there is an overpowering sensation of fingers reaching out that ever so slightly comes into contact with your skin. Your senses become raw with fear as you instinctively know that you have been touched despite there being nobody physically in sight.

Malevolent forces hover during this reign of terror, depriving you of rational thinking. Any last clear thoughts that you may have had prior to your personal contact with the other side are gone. Foul odors permeate the entire area at about the same time a mass of darkness blankets the humans experiencing the vile stench. The church grounds and cemetery are no strangers to floating orbs that sometimes appear to follow you through the highly spirited graveyard.

Claims from visitors who have walked around the area report that if you find the cemetery gates open that the ghosts and spirits are wandering freely, possibly to the grassy vacant lot just across the street where the log cabin and the Hankey Church once sat. Many feel that the area where the church was located is where the real paranormal activity runs at full speed day and night, while others claim that the entire area, including the cemetery is a hot spot for mist engulfed apparitions wreak havoc on the living who dare to enter the cemetery grounds.

The entire area was home to various members of the Hankey family. The Rolling Hills Golf Course now sits where the original homestead and the white farmhouse was once located. The old homestead can just barely be seen from the back side of the cemetery. At this location, many visitors to the cemetery have witnessed ghosts and spirits that appear in a fog like mist.

The strong smell of strawberries can sometimes be detected, wafting through the summer air. Just through the gate of the white picket fence, glowing tombstones can be seen just a few feet from the graves of Daniel and Catherine Best Hankey where they have been laying at rest since the early 1800s. Nearby, you will locate the grave of Revolutionary War soldier, Conrad Ludwig.

This is a highly charged area where ghost sightings are usually accompanied by bodily aches and joint pain, the sensation of heated skin and watery eyes similar to that of an allergy attack. Paranormal groups have attempted to debunk the supernatural activity that people claim hovers over Hankey Church Road near the cemetery, but the ghosts living there tell another story.

Location: Hankey Church Road & Beighley Road intersection, Murrysville, Pennsylvania.

Weston, WV, 2014: Our trip to the Trans Allegheny was one of our best encounters where paranormal activity is concerned. We found odd images in our photos, depicting unfamiliar faces in the background, and during our ghost hunt we had actual events that occured, leaving each of us with the knowledge that this place was definitely a ghost-riddled institution filled with a horrific past.

Never did you feel entirely alone besides the group of twelve that you were with throughout the tour. Disembodied whispers, footsteps and odd sensations were haunting reminders of the suffering that these humans endured in their daily life. Our son-in-law, Anthony had purchased a souvenir t-shirt on our way into the tour. By the time we walked through the exit door, the t-shirt had dissappeared from over his shoulder where it had laid during our entire time in the sanitarium.

The massive building known to locals as the Trans-Allegheny Lunatic Asylum with the grand architecture housing these lost souls can hardly be ignored, but visitors do not normally travel for miles to Weston to talk about the obvious features on the exterior of the haunted asylum. The West Virginia state facility was once the home to the state's mentally insane residents in an effort to make their lives better or so the medical professionals of the time so thought.

At times, you can see as they peer at you through the windows as you enter the door to their private hell. They follow you through the halls and scream out in desperation hoping that you may be the one who will finally release them from their prison. Tortured souls whisper in disembodied voices and cry out in anguished pain to the visitors that cannot always see them, and they beg for freedom to those who can.

You have just entered the saddest depth of hell you will ever witness...here you will enter a world filled by innocent victims who have been accused of being mentally insane, and although they are deceased entities from another time, they are very much still with us in spirit.

The larger than life building that features a massive clock tower directly in the heart of the hospital was constructed between 1858 and 1881, and is notably the largest hand-cut stone masonry building in North America, and is reported to be the second largest in the world, the Kremlin being the first.

The psychiatric hospital soon opened its doors in 1864 and ran its course up until 1994 when modern practices dealing with the mentally ill changed how they were to be treated. Updated facilities, medications, and counseling became the alternative treatment in favor of the inhumane practices of the past.

The Gothic revival design of the building then known as the Weston State Hospital lacked in warmth, but American architect and Confederate artillery commander Richard Snowden Andrews was enamored with the style and proceeded on with plans that would see it finished, no matter what the cost. The work was initially conducted by black prisoners, and later skilled stonemasons from Ireland and Germany were brought in for the finishing touches.

1864 would be the beginning of the torture that lurked within the walls of the massive rock building, and by the mid 1950's a staggering 2,400 mentally ill, along with drug addicts, alcoholics and epileptics were all living in crowded and unclean conditions.

Asbestos demolition contractor Joe Jordan from nearby Morgantown, WV purchased the deteriorated asylum and 300 acre-grounds at auction for a mere $1.5 million dollars in 2007, and immediately began maintenance on the property.

Unfortunately the tortured souls once housed within the walls of the inhumane estate are somehow stuck in limbo. Many of the residents simply did not belong in the facility and it is as if they are crying out this fact to anyone that will listen. The torture that must have been suffered from patients at the hands of inexperienced doctors that used little to no care is unthinkable by today's standards.

The medically untrained neurologist, Dr. Walter Freeman haphazardly performed ice-pick lobotomies and used electro-shock therapy with the idea that it would cure some of the patient's mental ailments. The amount of deaths that took place within the walls of the lunatic asylum were documented well into the thousands, which could very well be why the facility was named one of the most haunted places in the United States. Due to these reports of inhumane acts, owner Joe Jordan called in the TAPS team to do an evaluation of paranormal activity of the grounds.

Jason Hawes and Grant Wilson, founders of The Atlantic Paranormal Society aka TAPS, both warned against provoking the restless spirits of the asylum, because soon after the investigators began taunting the ghosts they begin to show signs of activity. Grant claimed that the old Weston State Hospital showed signs of "an intelligent haunting," meaning that someone who was once alive within the hospital is trying to communicate with those passing through in the present.

The Travel Channel took a closer into the vast amount of reports from visitors who claimed to have witnessed apparitions, strange noises and whispers while visiting the asylum. The results involved a seven-hour live broadcast, just in time for Halloween. It included their findings of the ghost sightings and extreme paranormal that exist at the Trans-Allegheny Lunatic Asylum.

Weston resident Sue Parker once worked at the asylum for 30 years as a psychiatric aide and in the admissions department. She claims that the fourth floor was haunted because she used to have to go up there after medical records, and that she could hear the spirits following her.

Ghost Tours: Heritage and ghost tours of the asylum run from March through October and cover an extensive part of the facility. The heritage tour covers the history of the facility and its patients along with the various wards and practices that would have occurred daily in the lives of the people staying there.

Details of the tour include medical procedures of that era, the civil war and a gold robbery that aided in West Virginia becoming a state. Touring all four floors is advised for the maximum benefit of the creepiness factor.

The ghost tours are the most popular and they are a ghost hunter's paradise. It is the most fun if you are into the questionable hobby of seeking out the paranormal. It entails a two hour grand tour of all of the reported hot spots, along with a view of how the mentally insane lived and died.

Visitors on these tours have reported thick air, the sound of squeaking gurneys being pushed, pressure, odd smells, cold spots, disembodied noises, whispering, screaming from the electro-shock area, and the feeling of being touched or pushed.

The most popular tour is the all-night public ghost hunt that starts at 9:00 p.m. and ends at 5:00 a.m. that is if you live through it without having a heart attack first. Groups of ten people are ushered through the darkest corridors and rooms in a bone chilling hunt for the liveliest spirits that they can find. If your mind doesn't run away with you then your tired body will.

A few reasons a normal functioning person could be admitted to the asylum from 1864 to 1889: Obvious laziness or a lack of motivation, egotism, the broken hearted, women with female diseases from depression to menopause, mental excitement, colds, physically disabled, sexually promiscuous, snuff, greediness, imagined female troubles, homeless, poor, gathering in the head, exposure and quackery, jealousy, religion, bad hygiene, asthma, bad habits and political excitement.

Remnants of the Past: Abandoned farms, a bake-house, and other out-buildings are located roughly a half mile from the main building, and a few surviving headstones remain intact. Other then the lively ghosts that are still roaming the hallways this is the only tell-tale sign of the people that once resided at the asylum.

The name Jasper Wyatt is clearly marked on a tombstone that is in fair condition, and is located in one of the three patient cemeteries found on the premises, however many of the graves are unmarked and void of markers symbolizing that anyone has visited in the **last decade.**

History

The Trans-Allegheny Lunatic Asylum was recognized as a Historical Landmark in 1990.

During the 1930s and '1940s, it is believed that Dr. Freeman performed more than 3,500 lobotomies.

The Trans-Allegheny Lunatic Asylum sits right in the heart of the town of Weston, WV

The month of October at the asylum features a Fall Fest and Witches Ball.

The Civil War wing is visited by a deceased soldier named Jacob.

Warnings from ghosts to leave the building have been heard by thousands of visitors.

Cameras and video equipment are welcome at the facility. Bring extra batteries.

Literature provided by the Trans Allegheny Lunatic Asylum indicated horrible conditions for the patients, and isolation from friends and family of the patients was strongly encouraged.

Location: 71 Asylum Drive in Weston, West Virginia.

Nemacolin Castle, October 2015: Magical, Medieval, enchanting, and built to defend against enemies, castles are one of the most fascinating structures on the planet. Some of the largest and most beautiful castles are located in Europe, but the United States has its fair share of these elegant fortresses that some people call home. A visit to Nemacolin during a Halloween tour a few years ago did not let us down.

We each experienced the sensation of being watched and as we walked through the interior of the antiquated dwelling. At several points during our tour, our group found that breathing became almost impossible and with this, the inevitable cold chills accompanied by a white mist would appear, the dissipate just as quickly as the eye captured it.

Nemacolin Castle is a Victorian landmark that is located in Brownsville, Pennsylvania. From the front rooms in the castle, visitors are given panoramic views of the Monongahela River. It was once the site of Old Fort Burd. The famous Nemacolin Castle was previously known by Nemacolin Towers.

The Tudor style estate dates back to the late eighteenth century. The castle was built by Jacob Bowman, who was appointed by George Washington as Brownsville's first postmaster. The castle was home to the

Bowman family for many years. Today, it is operated by the Brownsville Historical Society and is open to the public. Located at 136 Front Street.

Clairton, Pennsylvania, 2016: This one one of the few locations where we captured the image of a ghost in the window of one of the abandoned homes. Sadly, the neighborhood was demolished not long after our ghost hunt.

The mystery of the abandoned neighborhood of Lincoln Way in Clairton, Pennsylvania has been the subject of speculation since the early seventies, just after the first residents moved out, leaving all of their worldly belongings behind, including one vehicle, and then they simply disappeared without a trace. It is evident that something is amiss the second that you turn onto Lincoln Way.

It isn't the dead calm that is laced with eerie nothingness or even the homes that were once filled with families that are now completely void of all signs of life. The deprived yards, high weeds and belongings scattered along the entire length of the street are very real reminders that there is a history here that appears to be nothing more than a memory in time that offers not one clue as to what the past dealt to the people that once resided here.

Records from the tax assessor's office show details that the homes have had the same owners since the seventies, yet paid taxes have only occurred steadily with three of the homes to date.

Over the years, many people have questioned the sudden abandonment of Lincoln Way, and the answers have very from paranormal activity that includes a beast that dwells in the woods that surrounds the residential community from the now barricaded dead-end section of the street and the entire right side of the neighborhood.

Lincoln Way at first glance gives the feel of being dark and diabolical. The ugly ruins and debris make the entire neighborhood an eyesore and the perfect location for any red eyed beast to call home. Rumors concerning the abandoned and haunting neighborhood have resulted in many paranormal investigations that have varied results, depending on who you ask.

Coke piles emitting toxic fumes are situated directly across from the neighborhood awaiting workers to load the black solid carbonaceous material into railcars for delivery to the local steel mills, and located catty-corner from the Clairton steel mill on 837, the USS sign can be seen just across the Monongahela River from the entrance of the abandoned neighborhood. Many people speculate that the poor air quality back in the 60s and 70s could have led to declining health in the people and pets who lived so close to the valley's main source of income, making it a no-brainer to put this toxic neighborhood in their rear-view mirror.

Running along 837, just across the street from Lincoln Way, USS Steel's brightly painted green pipe is a constant reminder that the largest coke manufacturing facility in the United States is located just up the road. The steel mill has come under fire with the Environmental Protection Agency for violations concerning deadly pollution that posed health risks to local residents. The billowing white smoke coming from the stacks is always a source of concern for the town's people who live nearby even though clean air standards have been met and satisfied the strict requirements of the EPA.

The most recent paranormal investigation in March of 2015 gave mixed signals as to who or what has caused so many families to suddenly leave the place they once called home. Despite nearby 837 being a constant source of traffic, on this night, Lincoln Way was eerily quiet other than a few unexplained noises that emanated from the thick woods, just behind the homes.

Unexplained phenomena took center stage as the investigation progressed with flickering street light that continued in a foreboding pattern, snapping on and off as the group advanced closer to one particular house. Once we entered the home at 149 Lincoln Way, disembodied footsteps quickly became evident and the temperature dropped 15 degrees when standing in front of the home located directly in the middle of Lincoln Way. The investigators found that the second house located on the right side of the street sent the EMF monitor into a flux of activity that never ended until they completely walked off of the property.

What lies awake, lurking in this desolate neighborhood is anyone's guess. Looting and vandalism has added to the deeper elements of what you would expect to see in such extreme conditions where nothing is left except for the exposed remnants of days gone by. The dangerous sinkholes welcome unsuspecting strangers to come in closer for a look at what the deepest depths of hell has in store for them.

The silence sits heavily like a weight on your chest, beckoning those who enter the realm of of happy place that exists no more. The dark, eerie silence envelopes Lincoln Way, leaving unanswered questions as to what or who stands behind the deafening madness that drove sixteen families from their homes.

Not long after I wrote this article, the city of Clairton completely annihilated the entire stretch of houses that once sat on Lincoln Way. Today, the empty space on each side of street are all that remains of the haunted neighborhood.

Location: Lincoln Way, Clairton, Pennsylvania

Witchcraft is not something you should play with: Cold temps are fast approaching and the residents of Leonardtown, Maryland know that this can only mean one thing, that along with the freezing rain and snow, the curse of Moll Dyer will cast a dark shadow over the town's people yet once again. In 1697, Moll Dyer, a woman accused of being a witch simply because she survived the bitter cold without so much as a sniffle while most of the town's people were suffering from famine, hunger, disease, and eventually death, was forced from her only shelter and thrown out into the zero degree temps with only the rags on her back.

The colonists believed Moll Dyer to be a witch who had cast an evil spell over them. Irritated that she appeared to be of sound health while the rest of the citizens were meeting their demise by record numbers, Moll Dyer was pulled out of her home by the angry colonists. Fearing for her life she ran into the nearby darkened woods where she stood watching while the town's people burned down her only shelter. Witchcraft was illegal in the seventeenth century, and was punishable by death, so the colonists felt that this was their only recourse to eliminate the curse that they believed had taken over Leonardtown.

Moll Dyer fled the area in an effort to save her own life, all the while repeating strange words, promising to curse the very people who had sentenced her to her own cruel and inhumane death. Moll Dyer followed the creek until she could walk no more. Her body had become numb from the brutally freezing temps. Forced to slow her pace as hypothermia set in, she stopped to rest on a large boulder, kneeling down with one hand resting on the 875-pound rock and the other hand stretched out to the heavens.

Her frozen body was found in this very position by a young boy a few days later. When they removed her body, the colonists discovered that her fingerprints were embedded in the rock, confirming their allegations that she was in fact a witch that needed to die. They also realized that she had left behind a heavy curse that they could do nothing about as they watched one family member after another die a cruel death caused by starvation and illness which they believed to be nothing more than bad luck brought on by the old witch.

Today, the Moll Dyer Run that follows along the creek is considered one of the most haunted and cursed areas in Maryland. Anyone touching the rock is stricken with illness, shortness of breath and the feeling of being squeezed.

Moll Dyer Road today runs along the property where Moll Dyer succumbed to death and is witness to fatalities and unexplained automobile accidents despite it being a straight run road with no curves or blind spots. The owners now living on the property claim that they see dark shadows and ecto-mist resembling the outline of Moll Dyer.

The location of the cursed rock that Moll Dyer once perched on sits in the heart of Leonardtown at the St. Mary's County Historical Society building. The curse today is as strong as it was back when Moll Dyer first condemned the colonists and their descendants to the darkest depths of hell with nothing but bad luck following them into eternity.

Today, those who dare to touch the rock have reported the strange feeling of suffocation, almost like drowning and a case of bad luck that eventually subsides over time. The locals know that it is best to just walk past the rock as Moll Dyer's curse is just as strong today as it was over 300 years ago she she first cast it.

On March 27, 1697 the Council members of Maryland, during proceedings, commented on the bad weather, stating that "It hath pleased God that this winter hath been the longest that hath been known in the memory of man."

Calico: Nestled in the Calico Mountain's of Yermo, California visitor's will find the mining ghost town of Calico, located just 10 miles North of Barstow, California. Once popular for its Silver production, it has grown even more popular in recent years for its ghost town atmosphere and October ghost walk.

The get rich quick town was officially established on March 26, 1881, and word over the $86 million dollar silver strike spread like wild fire and soon hundreds of hopeful miners arrived and settled in, eventually raising the population to 1,200. The silver mining stayed strong until the late 1890's when the world value of silver fell to pennies on the dollar. Fortunately for the town of Calico, rich deposits of borax were also discovered in the Calico Mountains in the early 1890's, and with this new $45 million dollar discovery, mining still continued up until around 1910.

Once the town became vacant, Calico sat quietly barren from 1910 up until 1951 when it was purchased by Walter Knott of Knott's Berry Farm. He was easily able to envision the town as it once was, and set out to restore Calico to its original glory of the 1800's. He later donated the town to the County of San Bernardino which actively preserves and maintains the remnants left behind from days gone by.

Today, about a third of the adobe and wood buildings straddling the wooden sidewalks on the 480-acre parcel lot are originals. The rest of the buildings like the blacksmith shop, schoolhouse and the essay office, are all reproductions. Curiosity about the town's history draws in ghost town fanatics from everywhere. The ghost walk allows for the past to come alive and its colorful setting and natural surroundings make it ideal for passing the time away while enjoying a slow paced tour that highlights the best features of the town, then and now.

As you walk through the town you are automatically drawn to the window displays that are showcased in various buildings throughout Calico Ghost Town. The haunted town offers a wedding chapel that celebrates western weddings. Visitors walking the town will discover a mining company, an old schoolhouse, a bath & barber shop, a few mercantile shops and a handful of western eateries.

The most visited location in the town is located at the Town Hall building. The infamous "Character Hall of Fame" lists the colorful people who made of the town of Calico, and have not been forgotten. It would appear that Calico has come back to life and is operating at full steam as many different types of events are featured periodically through certain months of the year.

February in Calico: A piece of American History traditionally takes place in the historic silver mining town of Calico Ghost Town every Presidents Day weekend. This popular event gives visitors a glimpse of the north assaulting Calico as it is defended by the south. The town is occupied under martial law, and the sight of canon fortifications, hospital encampments, Robert E. Lee's makeshift headquarters and military drills make you feel as though you have really drifted back in a proverbial time capsule.

As you continue on your tour of the town you will likely come across Abraham Lincoln performing the Gettysburg Address while down the street a bit, General Grant and his troops arrive on train and by foot.

May in Calico: The Spring Festival, held during Mother's day weekend features bluegrass music, live entertainment, chuck wagon cooking demonstrations, a BBQ under the stars, and free flowers for all mothers.

October in Calico: The Calico Ghost Walk is a 90 minute after dark tour through the towns haunted ruins, and it has been carefully designed for guests of all ages. The tour is conducted during the last week of October, and includes a costume contest, pumpkin carving, and a walk through Chinatown and a tour of the Terror Silver Train. Tour guides give an in depth history of life in Calico during the 1800's, and they walk you past the haunted dwellings and share stories about the ghosts that have refused to leave their home. Sightings of friendly ghosts have been a regular occurrence since the late 1800's according to recorded documents, and word of mouth from the locals and quite a few unsuspecting visitors.

November in Calico: The Heritage Festival is held during Thanksgiving weekend and performances are non-stop, including an official visit from Santa himself. Everything from Native American dancing and the Medicine Man show to gunfights and street dancing take place during this eventful weekend. It is largely popular due to the many accommodations found at the ghost town. Restaurants, shops, camping, and wonderful scenery are all available year round.

December in Calico: Christmas in Calico has also become a popular event as the desire to see the holidays without all of the hype of commercialism gives the feeling of a time when life was simpler. The town is appropriately dressed for the occasion, and the seasons highlight is when the huge Calico Christmas tree comes to life with colorful lights on December 10th. One of a kind holiday gifts can be purchased at the local Calico gift shop that is ran by locals dressed in their western Yuletide garb.

Made in the USA
Columbia, SC
18 January 2023